ARCADIA

Title: Arcadia

Author: Direen, Eilidh

ISBN: 978-0-6457705-0-6 (print)

Subjects: YOUNG ADULT FICTION / Thrillers & Suspense; General / Dystopian / Science Fiction; Space Opera / Alternative History

Cover concept by Eilidh Direen.
IG: @eilidh.direen
Website: eilidhdireen.com

Cover design and layout by Heather Excell.

Dedication

To Daniel-san, who inspires me to write
and create things every day.

ARCADIA

EILIDH DIREEN

Part One

Chapter One

George LeVillain sat with his brothers and sisters in the darkest corner of the basement, waiting.

His father was having dinner with some important men upstairs and had bidden the children strictly to make no noise, nor to come out until they were told. If they listened intently, they could hear the muffled voices from the dining room, but it was impossible to discern what was being said, and none of them much cared to hear it anyway.

There were seven LeVillain children in all. Marcus came first, and he was sixteen; then Jacob, who was fifteen; then thirteen-year-old Genevieve. George was right in the middle, and he was twelve. Then came CJ (Catherine Jane), who was ten; then Jacinta, who was nine; and the last was Teddy, who was only six. All of them were small and pale and had bright red hair. They lived with their father, Raphael LeVillain, at the top of a tall green hill, in a narrow house without any windows. None of them had ever known their mother.

It was Jacob who first succumbed to boredom and began teasing the younger ones. "Hey, Teddy. Hey Teddy, guess what?"

"What?" demanded Teddy.

"There's a monster living in this basement, and he's *verrrry* hungry."

"No there isn't!"

"Yes there is."

"Is not!"

"There is, I've seen him."

"You're lying."

"His name is Phil."

"That's a stupid name for a monster," Jacinta cut in, as Teddy's bottom lip trembled.

"His name is Phil," Jacob continued, warming to his theme, "and he lives here in this basement and has slumber parties with the rats. He's always hungry, but he doesn't eat rats – only ratty little boys whose names begin with T——"

"STOP IT!" Teddy roared.

"Jacob, that's *enough*," said Marcus. "Apologise."

"I was only playing with him——" Jacob began – but was cut off as Marcus shoved him to the floor. "Oww."

"Apologise to Teddy."

Jacob gave an exaggerated sigh. "Sorry, Teddy."

George, watching the interaction play out, felt nervous and tried to listen to the voices upstairs, wondering whether they had heard anything. Nothing seemed to have changed, but he wished the others would take their father's warnings more seriously.

"Why don't we play a game?" Genevieve suggested.

"Okay," said Marcus. "A quiet one, though. No running. Let's play Mao."

"I don't think we should," CJ piped up from behind George. "Papa told us not to make *any* noise."

"He won't hear anything from up there. He's too busy talking – and anyway, we'll be quiet. Teddy, go and get the cards."

As Teddy trotted obediently off to the other side of the basement, where the toys were kept, George turned to CJ and whispered, "*I'm* not going to stay here and get in trouble. You can come and hide with me in the secret place if you want."

"Okay," she whispered back. And the two of them crept away through the maze of cardboard boxes and discarded bits of furniture to the 'secret place,' an old water boiler which had burst many years ago and was beginning to rust at the seams. It was 'secret' because from the front it still looked sealed, but if you went right up to it, you could see that the rust had eaten away at it from behind, leaving an opening just small enough for a child of George's size to crawl through. He had discovered it some months ago, and used it to win many a game of hide-and-seek before the others had cottoned on to his tricks.

George and CJ sat for some time in the secret place, listening as the game outside grew more and more heated – which they both knew had been inevitable. George could feel his sister trembling next to him, and wordlessly took her hand in his. It would be alright. No one would find them here, even if they did come looking. And afterwards, when the signal was given, they would come out again and everything would be –

SLAM.

Someone had thrown open the basement door.

Abruptly, the game stopped.

Clinging to each other in terror in the secret place, George and CJ could see nothing of what followed. But they could hear the voices of unfamiliar men outside: "And *what* do you call this, LeVillain?"

"Traitor!"

"You sick bastard, what have you done?!"

And then their father's voice, strained with panic: "You don't understand! *None* of you! I had to violate the sanctity of life in order to *protect* it, I——" There was a fleshy *thud*, followed by a groan – then some kind of scuffle – a piercing scream from one of the girls…and then, silence.

It was a long time before George and CJ dared venture out from the secret place. When they did, they found that the strange men had disappeared, taking their father and siblings with them.

Chapter Two

The first thing they did was search the house from bottom to top, to ascertain that they really, truly were alone. A thorough examination yielded zero trace of Raphael LeVillain, his progeny, or the men who'd come to visit. Finally, CJ sat down on the floor and wept. George, not knowing what else to do, knelt beside her and held her tightly.

"Where'd they go, George?" she wailed.

"I don't know."

"Well, what're we going to do?" Her tiny body shook with sobbing, and the tears trickling down her cheeks were beginning to soak through his jumper.

George thought for a moment. "We'll have to go and look for them."

CJ quailed. "Out of the house?"

"Yeah."

"But Papa said——"

"I *know*, but we can't just stay here. What if they don't come back?"

CJ was silent for a while, processing this idea. Finally, she wiped her eyes, nodded, and stood up. "Okay."

■

They took nothing with them save their coats, two backpacks full of food, and a portrait of their father which CJ had drawn on a page torn from one of Enid Blyton's *Faraway Tree* books, since there did not exist any photographs of Raphael LeVillain or his children anywhere.

George led CJ by the hand as they walked down the hill towards the distant city outskirts. It was twilight, and their already unfamiliar surroundings were distorted and terrifying in the deepening darkness. Strange black shapes loomed out at them on either side, reaching towards them with twisted, blackened limbs.

"What are those things, George?" CJ asked, pressing in closer to him.

George stopped and looked more closely at the nearest of the shapes. His brow furrowed. "I think… they're trees."

"*Trees*? Like they talk about in books?"

"I think so," George said, more decidedly this time. "They look a bit like that in the pictures in the *Faraway Tree* books."

CJ shuddered. "I didn't think trees would be so scary."

"That's just because it's dark. Everything looks scary in the dark; Papa told me that once. C'mon, let's keep going."

The sky turned darker as they walked, and the buildings around them multiplied, until finally they reached the bottom of the hill and were standing at the edge of the city. It was here that the children had to stop once again and consider their situation.

"*This* doesn't look like the cities in books," George said, frowning up at the view before them. What funny shapes and sizes these buildings were! And what strange materials they seemed to be made of! There were no bricks or mortar in sight, only cold, smooth surfaces which gleamed in the fluorescence of a hundred thousand artificial lights. And there were no motorcars – only sleek, dark, oblong shapes zipping soundlessly along the road without appearing to touch it at all. And the sounds everything made…! Despite having read voraciously for as long as he could remember, George hadn't any words to describe the sounds at all. Taken altogether, the sensory experience was overwhelming, and the children felt rapidly more disoriented as they continued on, deeper into the city.

George had thought hard about what to do once they cleared the residential area. He had the beginnings of a plan, but the obliquity of his surroundings was making him question everything he'd thought he'd known about the world. He'd felt confident on the way down the hill, but the further into the city they went, the harder it became to find anything around him to map his existing knowledge onto. But he could feel CJ trembling as she walked beside him, clinging onto his sleeve for comfort, and he knew he had to be brave and keep trying. Anyhow, there was one thing of which he was still certain. He'd read about it so often that even the absence of motorcars couldn't shake his faith in it – and that was that at times like these, the first place to go is to the police station.

The problem was, of course, how to get there. In every book George had read, people who wanted the police station generally knew already where to find it. But it had never occurred to him that he might need to go to the police one day, so he had never asked his father where he might find the station. And anyway, his father wouldn't have answered. (Raphael LeVillain seldom talked about the outside world, and when he did, it was in the form of myths and fables, not facts.)

So, in the absence of prior knowledge, what did people do when they needed to find something? They did one of three things: look for signage, use a map, or ask for directions. George was hesitant about the latter two options; he had never come across a map, and wouldn't know how to read one if he did. As for asking people for directions, well, his father had ordered him never to talk to strangers, and although the circumstances were dire, he wasn't going to break that rule if he could help it. That left only option number one.

George had never seen a real sign before, but he had an idea of what they looked like from the picture books he'd read in his infancy, and he was fairly confident that he would recognise the word 'POLICE' if it popped out at him from the exterior of some building or other.

"Keep a sharp lookout for a sign pointing to the police station," he told CJ, giving her hand a squeeze. "As soon as we find one, we should just need to follow the arrows, and we'll be there before you know it."

CJ sniffled. "I don't like the way the people are looking at us. Like we're nasty insects or something. It's scaring me."

"They're probably just surprised to see any kids out on their own this late at night. Just ignore them and they'll leave us alone. C'mon, help me look for a sign that says 'POLICE'."

"But what will we do when we get there?"

"I don't know exactly, but they'll help us. They always do in books."

"They don't *always*. In *Trixie Belden* the police just get cross at her all the time."

"That's 'cos she keeps getting in the way of their business. *We* aren't doing that. We just need help finding Papa and the others. Now keep looking!"

And keep looking they did, but to no avail. The labyrinthine streets grew narrower and more claustrophobic, and although the amount of signage did increase, there was nothing to indicate the presence of a police station anywhere. In the end, George was forced to reconsider his position on asking for directions, and turned to speak to the next person they chanced across: a woman who looked to be in her early twenties, wearing a smart blue overcoat.

"Excuse me——" George began – then faltered as the woman stopped abruptly in her tracks and looked him up and down with a shocked expression. He felt CJ grip him tighter, but that only strengthened his resolve. "Excuse me," he repeated gently, "we're looking for the police station. Can you please tell us where it is?"

"The police station?" the woman echoed, more calmly than her initial reaction had led the children to expect. Whatever it was that had startled her (perhaps it was simply that she had been deep in thought and wasn't used to being accosted by strangers – and after all, who would be used to that?), she seemed to have recovered from it. "What would you want to go there for?"

George was taken aback by the question. Surely people wanted the police for all sorts of things? But perhaps this woman had never needed them herself. Lucky for her if that was the case. "We've lost someone, and we need help finding him."

"Ah." The woman had lost all appearance of surprise, and was now regarding them with something very like amusement. "Well, you're going completely the wrong way. It's down that street, at the end, next to the old courthouse."

"I thought it would be more central," George said.

She laughed. "What for?"

George couldn't think of an answer, and after a moment the woman laughed again and continued on her merry way.

"George, why was that lady laughing?" CJ asked.

"I don't know. But it doesn't matter. We know where to go now, so let's go!"

■

The police station turned out to be located on the third basement level of a high, narrow building with very few windows. George couldn't tell what the rest of the building was used for, but he didn't care either. He kept a firm hold of CJ's hand as they rode the lift down beneath the earth, as much to comfort himself as her. The lift opened and they found themselves in a long hallway with several doors on either side. It was empty, so there was no one to bother them as they walked along it until they found the door marked 'POLICE'.

"Here we go," George whispered as the door opened with a slight hiss…to reveal nothing more than a small cubicle, a bit like a phone booth, with an odd shimmering panel set into the back wall.

"What is this?" asked CJ, as they squeezed with some difficulty into the cubicle and the door slid closed behind them.

George said nothing. It was taking all he had not to burst into tears of frustration. Why was *nothing* the way it was supposed to be? What had been the point of all those books if they had failed to teach him anything *useful* about the world? But he couldn't let CJ see how worried he was, or she'd start panicking, and he wouldn't be able to help her.

At that point, the panel on the wall flashed with bright blue light, making both children jump. Then words began to appear on it, as if by magic: 'PLEASE STAND IN FRONT OF SCREEN.'

"It wants us to stand in front of it," said CJ.

George frowned. "But we are."

"Well, it's very high up. Maybe it can't see us."

"How could a thing like that *see* us?"

"I don't know," CJ said stubbornly, "but if it wants people to stand in front of it, then it must have a way of telling if they're doing what it says, mustn't it? Here, let me get up on your shoulders so I can try to reach it."

Sceptical, but unable to think of any better ideas, George did as he was bid, and in a moment, CJ was leaning up against the wall, peering into the strange panel, while George fought to keep from tottering beneath her weight. She was small for a ten-year-old, but not *that* small.

"Is it doing anything?" he demanded.

"No, not – oh!" CJ broke off as the screen flashed again, and a voice, which seemed to come from everywhere around them all at once, began to speak.

"Please state your request," the voice said. It was impossible to tell if it belonged to a man or a woman, but it sounded calm and reassuring.

"What should I say?" CJ whispered.

"Say that we're looking for our papa and brothers and sisters," George hissed back.

CJ did as he said.

"Request not recognised," said the voice.

"What does that mean?" CJ asked crossly.

"Oh. It probably wants us to use proper names. Say Dr Raphael LeVillain has gone missing and we need to find him."

CJ did so, exhibiting the picture she'd drawn for further clarity. The voice replied, "Your request is being processed. Thank you. Have a nice day." And with that, the screen went dark.

The children were silent for a moment. CJ clambered down from George's shoulders. "What now?" she asked.

"Don't know," said George, stretching upright with a sigh. "We'll go back home, for now. I suppose they'll find a way to tell us as soon as they have any information." They turned towards the door, which slid open to let them back into the empty hallway.

"I don't want to go home," CJ said tearfully as they entered the lift. "It'll be so empty, and I won't be able to sleep not knowing where Papa and the others are."

"I know, CJ. I don't want to either, but what else would we do?"

CJ did not reply, and they rode the rest of the way in silence.

Then the lift doors opened, and they found themselves faced with two blank-faced young men in dark suits.

It was CJ who was first to notice that the men were not simply waiting to enter the lift, but were in fact staring intently at the two children. Wordlessly, one of them put out a hand towards her. Immediately sensing danger, she screamed, "RUN, GEORGE!" And before either of the men could react, the children had ducked around them and were sprinting out of the building into the street beyond.

Chapter Three

Blindly, they ran.

They could hear the shouts of the men behind them – raw pockets of noise piercing the already cluttered soundscape – and knew they didn't have long before they were overtaken. All thought of going home had left them completely. There was no telling who their pursuers were or what they wanted, but if they followed the children home, then home would no longer afford any safety.

George could feel his heart hammering against his chest. He'd never run this far or this fast in his life – had never had the space to do so even if he'd wanted to. It was only the adrenaline – the pure *terror* – that kept him going. Beside him, CJ panted desperately for breath, just barely managing to keep pace. People stopped and stared in bewilderment as they passed, but there was no time to worry about that now.

Instinctively, George knew that their only hope was to lose their pursuers in some sort of crowd – and that they had mere seconds to do so. He made a sharp turn and beelined for a long, low building which was buzzing with foot traffic. As the number of people in his peripheral vision increased, George ducked and weaved between them, taking full advantage of his smaller size to dart through the narrowest gaps, putting a little more distance between himself and his would-be captors each time he did so. CJ followed right behind him, moving fluidly through the throng, until at last they were inside the building itself.

It was built something like a train station, only there were no ticket desks or turnstiles. There were, however, several exits leading underground, which were labelled with what appeared to be platform numbers. Down the nearest of these fled George and CJ, dimly aware that they had moved far enough ahead of their pursuers that they would not be seen. A short flight of steps led them down to a deserted platform, alongside which was…well…it didn't *look* like any of the trains that George had seen in pictures, but what else could it be?

George stumbled to a halt, trying to fight the exhaustion that was finally setting in. His breath caught in his throat – ragged gasps echoing loudly through the platform chamber. His lungs were burning. Beside him, moaning faintly, CJ seemed to be in a similar condition. But they were alive, and they were alone.

Within a few moments, George had recovered enough to take stock of his surroundings. It was eerily quiet down here after the bustle of the city. There was no one about, not even a train guard. If he listened carefully, he could hear people up on the ground floor, and odd snatches of loudspeaker announcements which were too muffled to comprehend. At one end of the platform there was another of those shimmering panels fixed to a wall. It said: 'DESTINATION: MONS ARGAEUS. DEPARTS IN 00:03'. None of this meant anything to George; but he knew what they had to do next.

"CJ," he said quietly, "I don't know who those men were or why they were chasing us, but we're not safe from them until we get far away from here. So I think we should stow away on this train."

CJ looked up at him with wide eyes. "But what if we get caught?"

"We won't," said George, with more certainty than he felt. "We're good at hiding. That's why we're here in the first place, remember? Anyway, better to be caught by the train guards than by those men."

"But where is the train going? And what'll we do when it stops?"

"I don't know. We'll figure that out when we get there. Right now, the main thing is to get as far away as possible. Understand?"

"But——"

Footsteps began to sound at the top of the stairs.

"*Now*," George whispered – and pushed CJ through the open doors into the waiting train. Inside was a long aisle, on either side of which were a number of compartments, each with frosted glass windows and a little green light on the door which said, 'UNOCCUPIED'. Without stopping to consider, the children ran to the back of the train and darted inside the furthermost compartment. The doors slid closed behind them, and through the glass they could see that the green light had turned red.

"Does that mean no one will come in here?" CJ asked in a very small voice.

George shook his head. "If they're looking for us, this'd be the first place they'd look. We have to be smart about this." He looked around the compartment for somewhere to hide, but there were only two bench seats facing each other and a luggage rack up the top. There was also a window that looked out onto the wall opposite the platform, with two shutters attached. Frowning, he pulled the shutters closed and turned back to the door. When he took a step towards it, it slid open and the light went green again. He stepped back. It closed, and the light turned red. He looked closely at the latch, then said to CJ, "Give me that drawing you did of Papa."

Wordlessly, she handed him the piece of paper. He folded it in half several times, then stepped towards the door. It opened. Carefully, he wedged the paper inside the latch mechanism and stepped back. The doors closed, but not completely: a tiny crack remained between them...and the light stayed green.

They listened intently for the sound of footsteps, shouting, anything that might indicate their pursuers had followed them onto the train – but there was nothing. They began to breathe a little easier.

George flung himself onto one of the seats with a sigh. "That's as much as we can do for now."

"That was a clever idea," CJ said, admiration plain in her voice – though she kept her eyes on the door all the same.

He smiled wanly at her and said nothing. After the stress of the last few hours, he felt completely drained. CJ climbed up onto the seat beside him and laid her head against his shoulder, and he shifted to put his arm around her. George was close with all his brothers and sisters, but he'd always had a soft spot for CJ. She didn't try to push him around like the older ones did, but she didn't act like a baby either and try to wheedle him into doing things her way. She understood his ideas, and he understood hers. It was a mutually beneficial partnership.

Presently, there arose a tremendous rumbling noise, and the train began to shake. Nervously, George tightened his hold on CJ, but said nothing. He had never been on a train before, so he had to assume that this was normal. And if it wasn't… well, there was nothing he could do about it either way.

A moment later, the train pulled out of the platform and entered the dark tunnel ahead – or at least, George assumed that was what was happening, based on the motions they were experiencing. After a few minutes, he rose from his seat. "We'd better close the door properly, in case anyone else decides to wander in. Hopefully the red light means no one will bother us." So saying, he removed the folded paper from the door latch and sat back down – just as the train gave a lurch and seemed to pick up an incredible amount of speed all at once.

Taken by surprise, George was thrown back against his seat. The air around him suddenly felt thin – flat – hot – cold – then his ears popped, and it went back to normal. His limbs felt leaden and numb, and he began to sweat. Then, a minute later, something shifted deep within the walls and floor of the compartment, and he could move again.

"Open the window," CJ urged. "Let's see what's outside."

George did so – and let out an involuntary gasp: for they were not, as he had supposed, racing through the city at top speed, but were in fact hurtling upwards into the sky! "CJ," he said faintly, "this isn't a train…it's a rocket!"

■

Hours passed. The children sat and stared through the window, mesmerised by the majesty of the cosmos. At one point, a voice like the one they'd heard at the police station informed them that the dining area was open. But they felt safer remaining in their seats, and ate some of the food they'd brought with them instead.

They were quite alone. No one came into their compartment, nor did they hear anyone moving in the aisle outside. George discovered some buttons set into the wall; one of them caused soft instrumental music to play inside the compartment. It was a long time before either of them said anything.

Finally, however, CJ spoke: "George?"

"Yes?"

"How long do you think until we stop?"

George considered. "I don't know. Space is very big. But it can't be *that* long, or they'd have given us beds to sleep in, wouldn't they? We'll just have to be patient."

CJ nodded. "Okay."

Soon thereafter, she lay down on the seat beside him and dropped off to sleep.

George, equally tired (for it was well past midnight), but unwilling to risk being caught unawares, slapped himself a few times to stay awake, and turned up the music slightly. Turning back to the window, he gazed into the starry void and once again felt his breath catch. It was heart-achingly beautiful. When he looked at it, he felt a yearning that he couldn't articulate.

Soon, however, this feeling turned into a more tangible yearning for his family. Thus far, he had not allowed himself to dwell on the reality of his position, instead forcing himself to stay focussed on the next logical step to take. But now, with nothing to do except to wait, and with CJ sleeping soundly next to him, there was nothing to stop him from thinking about how much he missed his father and brothers and sisters, and how confusing the world outside was, and how small and helpless he felt in the face of it. And the more he thought about it, the worse he felt, and the more impossible his task appeared.

At last, overwhelmed by the enormity of his situation, George broke down and wept bitterly, until without willing it, he, too, slipped into sleep's soft embrace.

Chapter Four

He was woken by CJ shaking him. "George, wake up."

"Hm?" he said, blinking in confusion. Had the last twelve hours been a dream?

"George, we're landing!"

He sat bolt upright and looked out the window. Sure enough, they were descending towards an enormous landmass, atop which a gleaming city could be seen. As if on cue, the disembodied voice said: "Preparing for descent. ETA: 10 minutes. Please remain in your cabins."

So it wasn't a dream.

George sat numbly and watched as the city inched further into his field of vision. His sleep had been troubled, and he lacked the energy to feel anything any more, save a faint stab of curiosity about where they were headed. CJ, on the other hand, was glued to the window, her jaw hanging open in what was very nearly a smile. "Where d'you think we are?" she breathed.

He looked out towards the city – to the cold grey mountains beyond it – to the distant sun on the horizon. "I think…it must be the moon."

CJ said nothing, only gripped his hand in excitement. To be sitting in a rocket bound for a city on the moon was an experience that neither of them in their wildest imaginings had ever thought possible. There was something about this moment that, despite their recent suffering, filled them with pure joy and wonder.

A short time later, they touched down within the city limits and proceeded along a track that led into another station like the one they'd left from. The disembodied voice spoke again: "This shuttle terminates at: Mons Argaeus. Please collect your belongings and disembark. Thank you, and have a nice day."

"We'd better wait a few minutes before we get out," said George, "in case there's anyone else aboard. We'll let them leave first."

CJ nodded. "Do you think those men followed us in here?"

"I don't know, but we shouldn't risk it. Anyway, Papa told us never to speak to strangers, so I don't want anyone asking us questions about why we're travelling to the moon by ourselves."

So they waited, then, once they were fairly sure they must be the last remaining people aboard, they shouldered their backpacks, opened the compartment door and peeped into the aisle. It was empty, so they cautiously made their way to the exit and hopped out onto the platform. There were a few people outside, leaning against walls or sitting on benches, talking to each other, or reading, or listening to music. No one took any notice of the children as they ascended the stairs that led up to the concourse, much to their relief.

"I need the bathroom," CJ whispered as they climbed.

George nodded. "We'll look for one."

They entered the concourse, which was busy but not unbearably crowded. It appeared to be morning outside, and the building was pleasantly lit through enormous arch-shaped windows. It was very clean and well-decorated, and had a warm, friendly atmosphere – which puzzled George, who had always assumed that transit stations of this kind ought to be minimalist and functional in design. But right now, he had more important things to worry about. Mercifully, they found a toilet block off to one side. There was not a great deal in their father's library that had been written about public toilets, but the signage was clear, and when they entered the room, it was a fairly straightforward process, accompanied by jazz music playing from an unseen speaker system.

When they were each finished, they returned to the concourse and ducked behind a large pot plant so as not to draw unwanted attention while they planned their next move. "What we need," said George, "is a newspaper. We've reported Papa's disappearance to the police, which means the media should have heard about it by now. We should see if they've written anything about him in the news. They might know more than we do. Then we might get an idea of where to look for him and the others."

"But shouldn't we let the police do the looking?" CJ asked. "What if they get angry at us for interfering in their business, like in *Trixie Belden*?"

"We aren't going to interfere," George explained patiently. "But maybe if we knew a bit more, then we could figure out who those men were and what they did with Papa, and then we could help the police to find him faster. Anyway," he continued hurriedly, seeing that his sister wasn't entirely convinced by this logic, "what else are we going to do? We can't go home for at least a few days, in case those men are there waiting to catch us."

"I suppose so," CJ said, still looking doubtful.

"Also," said George, "we'll need weapons to defend ourselves in case we get chased again. Don't look at me like that——!" (as CJ's eyes widened), "——It's self-defence! Papa said it's okay to use a weapon if you're defending yourself or someone else. Now come on, let's go. There should be plenty of newspapers around here; train stations in books always sell them, so I don't see why a rocket station shouldn't." He strode out from their hiding place, looking, as always, more confident than he felt. After a pause, CJ followed him.

It proved, however, impossible to find a newspaper anywhere within the station. There were shops a-plenty, and cafés and restaurants, but nothing even remotely resembling a newsagent. They did, however, find a sports and hobbies shop which carried baseball bats and pocket-knives. CJ refused to take a knife, but reluctantly accepted a bat. It was here that they realised they hadn't brought any money with them. In fact, neither of them had ever seen, much less possessed, any money before. Their father had handled the household finances, and of course, they had never needed to buy anything for themselves.

"What do we do?" CJ whispered, as they stood uncertainly at the back of the shop with their as-yet unpurchased goods.

George thought for a moment, and was filled with grim determination. "Safety is the most important thing right now. We can ask Papa to send through a payment after we find him. Put the bat in your bag."

"But——"

"Come on!" And so saying, George slid the knife he'd chosen into the pocket of his own backpack. CJ obeyed, casting a worried glance at the counter. But there were no staff to be seen, and as they shuffled guiltily out of the shop, they attracted nothing more than a passing glance from one or two customers.

Armed thus, and having failed heretofore in his quest for a newspaper, George began to reconsider his position on asking for help. After all, he'd done so already once before, and it hadn't turned out that badly. Accordingly, he whispered his intention to CJ and scanned the concourse for a suitable grown-up to approach.

It was then, for the first time, that he was struck by how serene and unhurried the people in the station were. In every book he had read, people in cities – especially people riding on public transport – were depicted as frantic, harried, and self-absorbed, rushing about their business with vacant, downturned eyes. But these people were nothing of the sort. 'Cheerful' wasn't quite the right word for them…but they moved with a certain reassurance and placidity: they didn't quite walk in straight lines; their attention was directed outwards, drifting from one element of the environment to the next, as though they had all the time in the world. The sense of leisurely exploration he saw in them, in addition to the knife he carried, emboldened George even further, and presently, he selected a passer-by at random – a young man of perhaps eighteen or so, wearing a large floral shirt and a bucket hat – and stepped neatly into his path.

"Excuse me," said George.

The young man started violently, and blinked several times before saying anything. "Whoa, where did *you* come from?"

George wasn't in the mood to answer invasive questions. "My sister and I just arrived here, and we need a newspaper. Can you please tell us where to buy one?"

The man blinked again. "A news what?"

"Paper. We need – er, well, we want to know if there's anything in the news about a man who went missing."

"Oh. Well, do you know who it is? I can check the news for you."

George hesitated a moment, but decided that the man seemed trustworthy. "Dr Raphael LeVillain. He went missing yesterday."

The man did not appear to recognise their father's name, which was surprising. But he nodded and produced from his pocket a strange spherical device which was coloured to match the pattern on his shirt. Holding it in the palm of his hand, he tapped it with his thumb, and immediately there appeared hovering over it a small, semi-translucent creature that was somewhere between a mouse and a hedgehog in likeness. The children jumped with fright as it materialised, having never seen anything like it before. It did not, however, appear to be dangerous.

"Bepo," the young man said to it, "search all news sites for 'Raphael LeVillain'."

"Raphael LeVillain," the creature replied in an unnatural high-pitched voice. "'Renowned Scientist Arrested – Crimes Unknown.' Mercury Newscasting Corporation, uploaded 6 hours 24 minutes ago. No other results."

"Must be an exclusive," the young man said. "That means it's serious."

George fought to keep back a rising sense of panic. After all, he'd already known that his father and siblings were in trouble. "Can you find out anything more?"

The man shook his head. "If there were any more on the site, Bepo would have said so. What you want to do is contact the MNC and ask them to keep you informed as they uncover any new information. Although, they've shut down their remote public contact system, so you'd have to visit them in person."

"Alright," George said defiantly, "then where do we find them?"

The man squinted at him suspiciously. "You really *aren't* from here, are you? It's all in the name. You have to go to Mercury."

"You mean the *planet?*" CJ blurted out before George could stop her. She clearly hadn't worked out that it was unwise to let on how little they knew about the world.

"Yes, I mean the planet, what else?" the man said, annoyed. "You take that shuttle line over there. Now if you'll excuse me, I think I'm finished with this conversation. Have a nice day." And with that, he tapped his strange spherical device again and Bepo disappeared. The man stowed the device in his pocket and walked away at the same leisurely pace as before.

"That wasn't very polite," CJ said quietly.

George sighed. "No, it wasn't. But he did help us. And CJ, we can't act so surprised about everything people tell us. They think we're not normal, and I don't like that, so we have to pretend that we know how things work, but we're just not from this specific area. Okay?"

"Okay," CJ said, but he could tell she didn't really understand. And he couldn't explain it to her because he didn't really understand it himself: it was just a gut feeling. But the way that man had looked at them...like he thought something was wrong with them but couldn't really be bothered asking about it... It was very unpleasant to be regarded in such a way, and George had no desire to repeat the experience.

Still, at least the next step was before them. George took CJ by the hand and led her down to the platform which the young man had indicated. There were more people about the place this time, many of whom glanced curiously at the two children who were so obviously travelling on their own. But no one confronted them, and they found themselves a compartment on the shuttle without any trouble. It was slightly larger than the last one they'd been in, and the seats in it could be folded out into beds.

The journey lasted a few days (George lost track of how many), but was uneventful – even enjoyable at times. George and CJ kept to their compartment except for the odd furtive trip to the dining area for some food. They did not encounter any of their fellow passengers (for it seemed that everyone aboard was equally reclusive). For the most part, they simply sat and watched the wonders of space unfolding through the window before their eyes. It was an experience that did not require much talking, and so they spent a great deal of their time in silence: not the bittersweet silence of solitude, but the comfortable, intimate silence of communion.

■

At the end of their journey, George and CJ disembarked with a renewed sense of hope. The city they'd landed in was called Caloris. Its shuttle station was much larger than that of Mons Argaeus, and was built in a completely different style, down to the layout and interior décor – though still with the same warm, welcoming atmosphere. Upon entering, George wasted no time in asking for directions to the Mercury Newscasting Corporation, and was pleased to hear that it was only a few blocks away from the station.

As they were about to leave the building, George hesitated. What would it be like outside? How could human beings survive on a foreign planet? None of his books had ever explored the question – or at least not in any depth – and he knew nothing of Mercury save that it was the closest planet to the sun. Supposing they needed some kind of protective clothing, and without it they'd set one foot outside and be burned to a crisp?

But the people walking in and out of the station entrance seemed normal, and did not appear to be wearing or carrying anything unusual – not even sunscreen. So after a moment, George braced himself, checked to see that CJ was still beside him, and stepped over the threshold.

The sight that met them was breathtaking, like an oasis in the desert. The buildings of Caloris were made of smooth polished stones and metals that glittered in the sunlight, sculpted into intricate forms which did not quite match any shape that George had encountered during his brief studies in geometry, many of them culminating in domed ceilings and tall spiral towers. These architectural marvels were flanked on all sides by lush greenery and elegant statues and water fountains, looking for all the world like some Olympian paradise. The people in the streets meandered along with the same easy grace they had shown inside the station. Above them, the brightly shining sky was divided by a web of scarlet light beams into neat hexagonal sections, through which they could gaze into the sun beyond without hurting their eyes. Every so often, one of these hexagons would blink slightly as some piece of debris was blown into it by the solar winds.

George and CJ allowed themselves a moment to absorb the splendour before them, then hastened down the street in the direction they'd been told, until finally they reached the head office of the Mercury Newscasting Corporation: a large, globular building with two metal wing-like structures attached to it.

The children continued to attract odd looks from passers-by as they entered the building and strode purposefully up to the front desk, but they'd grown used to this by now, and did not let the unwanted attention deter them. There was no one attending the desk, but there was a large button on one side marked 'ENQUIRIES'. George pressed it – and took an involuntary step back as there materialised above it a small, semi-translucent sphere with two wings: a miniature of the building they were standing in…except that it also had two eyes and a mouth.

"Welcome to the Mercury Newscasting Corporation!" it addressed them in a surprisingly deep voice. "Please state your request."

George stared at it for a moment until it repeated itself. Then, slowly, he said, "My sister and I are looking for information about Dr Raphael LeVillain."

"'Raphael LeVillain,'" said the apparition. "'Renowned Scientist Arrested – Crimes Unknown.' Uploaded 4 days ago. Further details to follow."

"That's *it*?" George demanded, frustration finally getting the better of him. "Don't you people know *anything*?"

"Further details to follow," the apparition repeated cheerfully.

George leaned against the desk with a heavy sigh. "That's it, then," he said to CJ. "Dead end. We might as well go home now."

CJ said nothing, but looked up at him trustingly and gave his hand a squeeze.

"Thank you. Have a nice day!" the apparition said.

They turned to leave – and promptly collided with five men in dark suits who glared down at them without speaking a word.

Instantly, George's knife was in his hand.

He didn't know much about fighting, beyond the basic self-defence training which his father had given him since he was four. But in this moment, he forgot everything he'd been taught – in fact, his mind seemed to stop working altogether. He felt a guttural howl escape his lips as he rushed at the nearest of the men and swiped blindly at him with the knife.

The man, clearly unprepared for the attack, stepped back too late, and the blade caught him inside his open jacket, tearing through the white shirt beneath and drawing a thin line of red above his hip. He gave an exclamation – sounding more surprised than pained – then paused, as if trying to re-evaluate the situation. One of the others made a grab for George, whose momentum had carried him past the first man and onto the floor. But George rolled out of the way and scrambled back to his feet. A third came at him, but jumped back as he jabbed with the knife. At the edge of his vision, he could see the other two moving in on CJ. She swung at them with her bat – missed – and cried out as one of them tackled her to the ground.

Enraged as well as desperate, George screamed again and launched himself at the first man he'd attacked. But this time, the man was ready for him and countered with a vicious blow to the elbow which knocked the knife out of his hand. Stunned by the pain, George staggered backwards. At that moment, he noticed that although the man's shirt was torn and there were traces of blood on the material, the wound beneath had vanished.

George had only a tenth of a second to feel confused by this before two of them grabbed him from behind and he was forced onto the floor, his arms pinned and a knee grinding into the small of his back. Tears pricked at his eyes – whether from pain or from anger he couldn't tell – and he choked down a sob as he twisted to look for his sister.

"CJ!" he yelled. "Are you okay?"

"Yes," she answered – but he could tell from the sharpness of her breath that she'd been badly hurt.

Furious, he struggled to break free, but his captors were too strong. "Let us go!" he screamed. "We've done nothing wrong – just leave us alone!"

For the first time, one of the men spoke. It was the man George had first attacked. "Get them out of here," he said.

The man's refusal to acknowledge him was too much for George, and as he and CJ were dragged roughly to their feet and marched out of the building, he broke down and wept with fear and rage.

Chapter Five

A short journey in a strange flying vehicle brought them to their destination: a great golden monolith of a building which was nearly impossible to look upon, so brightly did it reflect the sun's rays. George and CJ were escorted roughly inside, down a hallway and a flight of steps, into a small room containing two sofas facing each other, with a table in between.

Three of the men who'd captured them had disappeared, leaving only the one George had stabbed, and another with sandy hair. The first man looked sternly at the children and pointed towards one of the sofas. "Sit."

Not wanting to obey, but too frightened to do otherwise, George and CJ sat.

Rather than following suit, the two men remained standing between the children and the door. A long pause ensued.

Finally, the first man spoke again. "Where did you come from?"

George did not answer immediately.

CJ was more forthright. "Are you the police?" she demanded.

The man glared at her. "I said, *where* did you come from?"

George laid a hand on his sister's arm. "Earth."

"How did you get here?"

"We took the shuttle."

"That's not what I——"

George interrupted him. "Look, why should we answer your stupid questions? Who *are* you? Why'd you bring us here? We haven't done anything wrong, we're just looking for our family."

The man's mouth made a thin, straight line. "Your family?"

"Yes, our papa and brothers and sisters. They're missing, and we're trying to find them."

There was another pause. The two men exchanged a look that George couldn't understand. Then the one with sandy hair spoke. "Who is your father?"

George said nothing. He did not want to talk about his father's arrest, for there was no telling who these men were, or what they might do if they found out that he and CJ were the offspring of a man accused of 'crimes unknown'.

The first man looked directly at George and gave a cold, humourless smile. "Is it Raphael LeVillain?"

George remained silent. But he was not used to lying, and his face gave him away.

The man's smile broadened. "As expected." He turned to his partner. "Notify Kingsley. I'll handle the rest." The sandy-haired man nodded and left the room.

"What are you going to do now?" CJ asked quietly.

The man turned to look at her. For a moment – just a moment – it seemed to George as though his expression softened. But it was only a moment, and it could have been George's imagination. The man opened his mouth – then, before he could say anything, there was a tap on the door from outside.

The man frowned and went to the door – then, as it opened, his body spasmed violently, and he collapsed to the floor.

George and CJ leapt to their feet, unsure what was happening, and knowing they had no way to escape. Their astonishment increased as through the door stepped three children – two boys and a girl – clad in sleek black uniforms of a foreign material and design, and carrying equally unfamiliar weapons, which were silver and bore a vague resemblance to the hand pistols George had seen illustrated in his father's *Tintin* comics.

The eldest, a blonde boy of fourteen or so, grinned at them, showing slightly crooked teeth. "Hi," he said. "I'm Ajax, and this is Tim and Sophie. We're here to rescue you."

■

In a locked room, a man sat tied to a chair. He did not speak, nor attempt to break free from his restraints. There was no one else in the room with him.

There were no visible signs of harm on the man's body. His expression was blank. There was nothing to indicate that he had been mercilessly tortured for the past thirty-six hours, save for the emptiness in his eyes and the twitch at the corner of his mouth.

A stretch of time passed. The door opened and a second man entered. He was tall, and wore a white velvet suit and matching overcoat. The man in the chair did not look up.

"So," said the man in white velvet, "why did you do it?" His tone was light, almost friendly.

The man in the chair said nothing.

If the man in white velvet was irritated, he did not show it. "Well, Raph? Why would you do a thing like that?"

Twitch. "You know why, Aidan."

The man in white velvet shook his head. "Yes, I remember your little spiel as though it were yesterday——"

"It *was* yesterday."

The man in white velvet gave a very slight frown. "No, *before* that. We had this argument years ago. I didn't accept your reasoning then, and I do not accept it now."

Twitch. "Then I don't know what to tell you, Aidan."

A pause.

The man in white velvet stepped forward and bent so that he was level with the prisoner's lowered gaze. Two sets of empty eyes met. When the man in white velvet finally broke the silence, it was with little more than a whisper. "There are ways of undoing what you are, Raphael."

For the first time, something moved beneath the emptiness. "The Genesis Circle?"

The man in white velvet nodded. "Rumour has it they've succeeded."

Another pause, shorter this time. "And what does that mean for your Arcadia?"

"The question," smiled the man in white velvet, "is what does it mean for *you*?"

The man in the chair lifted his head. His eyes were clear and burning. "Please, Aidan," he whispered. "Let me go. It's been so long…"

The man in white velvet kept smiling. "I don't think so, old friend. I have a much better idea."

As he spoke, he turned towards the door and gestured. It opened. In came stumbling a teenage boy, who had obviously been pushed. The door closed, and the boy caught himself and straightened. He was blindfolded, and, from the sound of his breathing, terrified.

The prisoner jerked forward in his chair. "Marcus!"

The boy went still. "Papa?"

The man in white velvet smiled. "A touching farewell."

He drew a pistol from the pocket of his coat and shot the boy through the head.

"NO!" the prisoner screamed as his son crumpled to the floor.

The man in white velvet did not look at the body, but instead turned the pistol over in his hand, as though he'd never seen one before. "A rather inelegant weapon," he remarked, while the prisoner behind him began to weep. "Outdated. But you never can tell what may come back into fashion when the need arises."

He turned to the door and gestured. "Send in the next."

Chapter Six

"So where are we going?" George asked breathlessly.

The five children were running through the streets of Caloris, drawing curious stares after them as they went. Ajax led the way; then went Sophie, who was small and fast and had long black hair which streamed behind her like a banner; then George, who kept tight hold of CJ's hand; and bringing up the rear was Tim, who George guessed was Sophie's brother.

Ajax did not look behind him as he answered: "Space bridge."

"What bridge?" CJ panted.

"The space bridge. It'll get us home faster than a shuttle. C'mon!" He gave a whoop and jumped a fence that bordered a park lined with huge, sprawling trees, sloping gently down towards the edge of the city centre. The others followed.

George thought furiously as they ran. He had no idea who these children were, or why they were helping him, or where 'home' was, or what a space bridge might be. But it was clear to him that, as before, he and CJ needed to put as much distance between themselves and the strange men in suits as they could. When they stopped somewhere safe, he could consider the situation more carefully and formulate a plan from there.

So, putting all other questions out of his head, George ran.

As they cleared the park and went deeper into what seemed like the industrial side of the city, George noticed something odd about the way his rescuers moved. They were fast, but they did not give the impression of being chased. There was a fierceness and purpose in their stride, but beneath it there was confidence and joy, an exuberance that George had never observed in anyone before. It was invigorating to see, and he felt himself picking up his own pace to match them.

By and by, they came to a wide gravel yard filled with heavy machinery, some of which George vaguely recognised, some totally unfamiliar, all of it polished and well-kept. At the centre of the yard there was a landing pad of some sort, on top of which stood a vast metal archway that hummed with an invisible energy. George had never seen anything like it, but since they were moving covertly towards it, he could only assume that this was the space bridge.

The children slowed to a cautious trot as they approached the archway. There did not seem to be anyone about, nor were any of the machines in the yard in use. Nonetheless, there was a tacit understanding that they were not supposed to be here, and would undoubtedly be stopped if anyone happened to catch them.

"Put these in your ears," said Sophie, handing George and CJ each a pair of strange-looking metal studs.

"What are they?" asked CJ.

"They're to hold you together on the bridge, so you don't fall apart into atoms." She looked at them seriously, but did not offer any further explanation. George and CJ did as they were bid and inserted the metal studs into their ears. They felt cool, but not unpleasant.

Meanwhile, Tim had walked up to the base of the archway and was tapping the surface of a shimmering panel that was affixed to it. Ajax stood next to him and kept watch.

After a few moments, the boys turned and beckoned the rest of them onto the pad. "Bridge'll open in thirty seconds," said Tim.

"How does it work?" George asked.

"You just enter your destination and step through the gate when it activates," said Ajax. "You have to know the activation code, though. Tim's the best at keeping track of which codes you use for which gates."

"No, but how does it *work*, I mean? How does it get you from one place to another? It doesn't have any wheels, or engine, or – or *any*thing."

Ajax frowned. "Oh... I don't know. We just use 'em. We don't need to know how they work."

George was disappointed by this explanation, and might have argued with the other boy, except that at that moment the archway was filled with a piercing light, forcing him to step backward and shield his eyes with his hand.

Tim nudged him from behind. "Don't worry. It's safe. Just walk through it!" And with that, he followed his own advice, stepped through the archway, and vanished. Sophie went next, leaving Ajax to watch as George took CJ by the hand, drew in a deep breath, and entered the space bridge.

A sharp vibration shot through their bodies for a fraction of a second – and then they found themselves standing on the other side of the landing pad…only, it was a different landing pad, because the city around them had changed, as had the sky above it. They had arrived on an entirely different planet.

As George registered all this, the light flashed behind them and Ajax appeared.

Disoriented, George whirled around to look at the archway behind him. It was a different size and shape to the one he'd stepped through, and the light had vanished so that he could see through the archway to the unfamiliar cityscape beyond. His heart was racing, and he felt nauseous, but otherwise it was as though he'd simply taken a step forward. He checked to make sure CJ was alright: she grinned up at him with barely contained excitement.

Lost for words, George turned to Ajax, who smiled. "Welcome to Mars. This is my home town, Olympus Mons. Our base is just a few blocks from here. Follow me and we'll explain everything when we get there. Come on!" He gave another whoop and took off running again, with Tim and Sophie close behind him.

George looked at CJ. She laughed and pulled at his hand. "Let's go!"

∎

The 'base' turned out to be a hidden basement level of the Olympus Museum of Astronomy, which they accessed through the sewage system. Inside, George and CJ were astonished to find it well-lit, furnished, carpeted, and…occupied. There were four other children awaiting their arrival: two boys who could only be Ajax's brothers, and a much younger boy and girl who were obviously twins. They all wore the same black uniform as Ajax, Sophie, and Tim, though with varying degrees of neatness.

As George and CJ entered in the company of their rescuers, the strangers gave a cheer. The older boys rushed forward to hug and congratulate Ajax and the others, and the little children danced about the room, singing, "We found them! We found them!"

George and CJ stared mutely, too astonished to move or speak. Eventually, the tallest of the boys remembered his manners and greeted them with a big smile and a handshake. "Welcome to the family," he said. "I'm Dragan Smith, and this is my brother, Hugo." The other blonde boy nodded. "You've met my other brother, Ajax, and Tim and Sophie Moran. The little ones are Ruby Moran and Lewis Moran. What are your names?"

George hesitated. The children seemed friendly, but they were still strangers. And he had no idea what was going on. But he was no good at lying, and if things turned bad one way or the other, it probably wouldn't matter if these children knew his name. So he answered, "I'm George."

"And I'm CJ," his sister said, peeping out from behind him. "George is my brother."

Dragan smiled at her. "I could be your brother too, if you wanted. We all could be your brothers and sisters. We're one family here."

CJ looked up at him, eyes widening in confusion and shock. Her bottom lip began to tremble. "But...I don't *want* a new family. I want our old one back. I want Papa and Marcus and Jacob, and, and Gen and Cinty and Teddy..." She hid her face against George's chest, and he held her tightly, knowing she hated to cry in front of anyone.

"She didn't mean that to hurt your feelings," he told Dragan, who was clearly taken aback by this reaction. "But she's right. Our family was taken away, and we've been looking for them for days. We can't just find ourselves a new family and forget about them."

At this, Dragan's eyes darkened. He motioned for the other children to disperse, which they did, drifting away to various nooks and crannies to chat with each other or play games or undertake mysterious tasks of their own. Then Dragan ushered George and CJ into a side room with a table and several armchairs. The three of them sat, and Dragan gave them a long, calculating look.

"Listen," he said, "I'm sorry. I shouldn't have said it like that. We were all just so excited to see you... Anyway, it doesn't matter. You don't have to stay here if you don't want to. But you should know that it's not safe for you out there. If people see you, sooner or later Kingsley's agents will come after you again, and we might not be able to help you next time."

"Why *did* you help us?" George asked. "And who is this Kingsley person? Why aren't we safe outside? And why——?"

"Hold on, let me answer," said Dragan. He took a deep breath, as though deciding where to begin. "The reason we helped you is because the same thing happened to us. Ajax, Hugo and I lost our dad three years ago. We used to live not far from here, and one day, he told us some people were coming to the house, and that they were dangerous and we mustn't let them find us. He gave us a map to find this basement, and told us to stay here until he came for us. But he never did. So we stayed here, the three of us, hoping one day he'd come back. We made it our base. At first, we didn't leave, because Dad told us never to go outside or talk to anyone. But eventually we had to. We can't get packages delivered here, so when we need food or clothes or anything, we have them sent to a nearby depot and we sneak out there to collect them. And after a while, we learned how to get around outside without being seen——"

"But what's so bad about being seen?" CJ interrupted. "Why are people always staring at us like there's something wrong with us?"

"I'm getting to that bit," Dragan said patiently. "It's hard to explain quickly. How much do you know about the world outside? What did your dad tell you?"

George thought for a moment. "Not very much. He told us it was dangerous, and that we should never go out of the house or speak to anyone we didn't know."

Dragan nodded. "Ours said the same."

"We learned a lot from books, though," George said, a bit defensively. He knew he was ignorant about a lot of things, but he didn't want anyone to think he was stupid either.

"What books?"

"Well…storybooks, mainly. *The Famous Five. Trixie Belden. Anne of Green Gables…*"

Dragan shook his head. "Never heard of them. When were they published?"

"I don't know, I didn't think about stuff like that," George sighed. "They must have been pretty old, though. Hardly anything they talked about seems to be the same in the real world."

"What about the omnicon? Did you have access to that?"

"The what?"

"The omni-connect. It's a collection of information systems, like every book ever written all collected in one place. But you can do lots of other things with it besides reading. Your dad would have known about it. Did he ever show you his udev?"

"No-o…" said George, wishing desperately that he knew what all these words meant.

Dragan sighed. "Never mind, that's less important. Listen, do you know about the Arcadian Empire?"

George, feeling more and more useless by the second, shook his head miserably.

Dragan must have sensed his shame, for he smiled gently and put a hand on George's shoulder. "It's okay. Our dad didn't tell us much either; I think he wanted to protect us in some way. Yours must have been the same. Anyway, when our dad sent us here, he gave us a udev, which is what you use to look on the omnicon for information. That's how we found out about the Empire.

"See, years ago, before people left Earth and colonised the solar system, there was a man called Aidan Kingsley, and he discovered a way to stop himself from dying. No one knew how he'd done it, but they all wanted in on it. But he wouldn't share it with anyone unless he really trusted them, so all these people started trying to impress him and win his confidence, and eventually he became ruler of the whole Earth. But he still didn't share his secret with anyone except his most trusted friends, who he put in charge of everyone else. Then over time, as all the normal people lived and died, Kingsley and his friends stayed alive. And when people discovered space bridges and terraforming and began to live on other planets, Kingsley and his friends ruled those new societies as well. They called themselves the Arcadian Empire, and they're still in charge of everything today. No one dares stand up to them, because they can't be permanently hurt or killed – and anyway, most people still hold out hope that one day they'll earn Kingsley's trust and be given the secret to immortality themselves."

George gave an involuntary shiver, remembering the man he'd attacked, who had healed from the knife wound so quickly. "Are these the same people who took our families away?"

"We think so."

"But why?" CJ asked, beginning to tear up again. George didn't blame her. After all, what was more frightening than a kidnapper who couldn't be hurt?

"Well, that's the part we're not too sure about," Dragan admitted. "I think our parents must have done something to upset Kingsley, so he sent his agents to arrest them. There was nothing on the news sites about my dad, since he wasn't a public figure. But the Morans' parents were pretty well-known academics, so when they were arrested a year ago, it was in the news. Nothing about the crimes they'd committed, of course – but when I read about it, I had a feeling it was similar to what happened to Dad. And by that time, me and my brothers had figured out how to tap into the police data network, so when Kingsley's agents put out a wanted notice for Tim and Sophie and the twins, we knew they were being targeted because of their parents, and we decided to rescue them and bring them here.

"Then, about a week ago, we found out that Dr LeVillain had been arrested and Kingsley's agents were looking for two of his children – that's you two. They didn't know your names, but they had photographs and a last-seen location: Caloris. Then when they took the information off the network, we guessed that you'd been captured, and I sent Ajax and the others to help you. We want to do everything we can to interfere with Kingsley and his agents, to show them that they're not the boss of us. We call ourselves the Mortal Corps, because we're proud of what we are and we don't care about earning his stupid immortality. As long as he's hunting down dissenters, we'll be around to rescue them. And one day, when we're big enough and strong enough, we're gonna make him pay for everything he did to us."

Dragan's eyes went hard, and he stopped for a moment before taking a deep breath and finishing. "Anyway, my point is, now that you've escaped, your pictures will be up on the omnicon again. If anyone recognises you, they could alert the Empire in less than a second. Kingsley's agents would be after you immediately, and the whole goose chase would start again. You're not safe out there on your own, but in here, you are. Do you understand?"

There was a pause as George and CJ digested all this information. George's head was spinning. A thousand questions ran circles around the inside of his head, before being crushed to a halt by his growing sense of defeat. He didn't want to believe that anyone could be immortal, much less an immortal bent on controlling the rest of the universe. But he couldn't deny what he'd seen back on Mercury either. And regardless, if what Dragan said about the omnicon was true, then the only thing keeping him and CJ safe outside was the number of people who, it seemed, were ignorant or indifferent to what was going on in the world. But he couldn't count on everyone to be that way. And he shuddered to think what those men might have done to him and his sister if Dragan's family hadn't come to help them.

At last, he looked up at Dragan and spoke, doing his best to keep his voice steady. "If we stay with you, will you help us find our family?"

Dragan smiled and clapped him on the shoulder. "Of course we will, George." He stood and gestured towards the door. "But first, come and join us for dinner."

Despite himself, George smiled back.

■

Dinner consisted of slow-cooked beef, beans, and rice. During the meal, they talked of small things; there was an unspoken rule against asking overly personal questions. Instead, the nine of them spent the evening sharing jokes and stories, discussing the ins and outs of everyday life on Mars, and forming the beginnings of a plan.

Dragan and the Mortal Corps were perfect hosts. They asked enough about George and CJ to demonstrate care and investment, yet avoided saying or asking anything that would bring back painful memories of missing family members. They kept the conversation light-hearted and lively, but refrained from joking among themselves in ways that might exclude their guests. By the end of the night, even George, weary and suspicious as his recent experiences had left him, felt warm, welcomed, and relaxed by the courtesy of his rescuers. He even began to wonder if his father's rule against talking with strangers could be as universal as he had always supposed.

He and Tim had a moment of jubilant camaraderie upon discovering their mutual love of *The Phantom Tollbooth*, a book that George, more than any of his siblings, had always felt a particular resonance with. For all the unfamiliar talk of omnicons and udevs and terraforming and whatever else, it was nice to know that there were still some common points of reference between him and these wild runaway children.

The night wore on, and as they grew more comfortable with each other, CJ, who had mostly kept quiet until this point, gave voice to a question that had evidently been on her mind for some time: "So, why do you all wear matching clothes?"

"It's a uniform," Ajax said. "We belong together, so we show that by the way we dress."

"People out there have no concept of togetherness," Dragan added, stabbing at his beans with his knife. "Have you noticed that? They all dress completely differently from one another. Their udevs are calibrated to their own specific preferences – no two udevs are designed or operated in the same way. No two people act or look alike. It's like they hate the idea of belonging."

George and CJ had no idea what to say to this, so they nodded politely and focussed on their food.

"We can make uniforms for you too, if you want," Ajax offered, smiling shyly at them. "The twins make them for us. They're great at sewing." At the corner of the table, Ruby and Lewis beamed at the compliment.

CJ nodded sagely. "Our papa's very good at that too. He makes all our clothes." As soon as she'd spoken, she paused, clearly regretting having broached the subject of their papa.

"Does he?" Ruby asked, leaning over to touch CJ's sleeve. She examined the seam closely, then nodded. "He does a good job."

George saw the corner of CJ's mouth begin to droop, and hastened to move the conversation in a more productive direction. He turned towards

Dragan and asked, "So how are we going to find him and the others?"

Dragan, halfway through a mouthful of beef, nodded and chewed. After a second, he swallowed and said, "I've already got Hugo looking into it." It was then for the first time that George noticed Hugo's absence from the table; from the little time they'd spent with him thus far, he seemed significantly quieter than either of his older brothers. "We can access Kingsley's message banks through the omnicon," Dragan continued, "so if there's anything on there about where your family might have been taken, we'll know."

"Message banks?"

"Conversations he has over the omnicon with his officers." Dragan smiled. "It's sort of like reading his letters, or tapping his phone line. Do you know about telephones?"

George flushed and looked down. "I've read about them." He knew the older boy was trying to be helpful, but he didn't like the feeling of being talked down to. "Is it difficult to do? Reading his message banks?"

"Well, yes and no. Kingsley doesn't expect people to resist him, so he doesn't bother much with security. That's how come we rescued you so easily. But because of the way the omnicon is designed, people's message banks are always encrypted, so you can't just go in and read whatever you like. Given enough time, we could probably break the encryption, but even Kingsley would be sure to notice if we spent that long in his system. So it's easier if we know exactly what information we need – in this case, your father's whereabouts – so we can just get in, run a quick search, copy the information, get out, and decrypt the information offline at our leisure. If it were easier, we'd spy on him every minute of the day, and then we'd stand a better chance of defeating him."

George had only understood about half of what Dragan had said, but he'd had enough of seeming ignorant and did not ask for further explanation. Instead, he said, "That still sounds like a big job for one person."

Dragan shrugged. "We only have one udev. It's a special design that our dad modified so it couldn't be traced back to us, or we'd have ordered more by now. But Hugo's the best at scouting the omnicon, so I don't think we'll be waiting long."

While they waited, Dragan set the other children to clearing the table and washing up, while he took George and CJ on a brief tour of the Mortal Corps' base. It was all one floor, broken into three main sections: the common area where they'd eaten, containing tables, chairs, couches, and a kitchenette in the corner that had been adapted for twofold use as a kitchen-laundry; the living quarters, comprising a toilet block and a number of tiny rooms that had once been intended for private study, but which now contained camping beds and various personal items accumulated over months and years of occupation; and the 'workshop,' comprising three small office spaces which the Corps members split between them for work and play. George could see Hugo sitting in the corner of one room, fiddling idly with what could only be the famous udev. It was about the size of an apple, and split into a number of triangular blue panels which could be arranged in different configurations.

At the end of the workshop, outside the furthermost office, was a locked metal door, rusty from years of disuse. This, Dragan explained, had once led up to the museum; but it had been so long since this basement had been in use that most people had forgotten its existence. The only way to get in or out now was the hidden entrance through the sewers, which was located at the edge of the common room furthest from the kitchen.

When they came back around to the common room, they sat at one of the tables and played cards for a while. George was unpleasantly reminded of how his brothers and sisters had played Mao right before they were caught, but he was too polite to ask to do something else. He glanced anxiously at CJ, but she seemed to have cheered up since dinner, and if the card games bothered her, she gave no indication of it.

By and by, Hugo emerged from the workshop.

"Found 'em," he said.

Chapter Seven

Twelve hours later, Dragan led a small crew out of the space bridge and into the heart of Arcadia, capital city of Earth. Their destination: King's Castle, the great central fortress from which Aidan Kingsley ruled the peoples of the solar system. It looked nothing like any of the castles George had seen in pictures; it was a high tower with only three walls – a gigantic triangular prism reaching up into the heavens, extending far beyond the rest of the city skyline. Surrounding it were gardens and courtyards and fountains, much like those on Caloris, only vaster and grander.

The group consisted of Dragan, George, CJ, Tim, and Sophie. Ajax had remained at the base to keep an eye on the twins (who were too young) and Hugo, who was asthmatic and not a very fast runner. Originally, CJ was to have stayed behind as well – and to her credit, she had not protested. But George had seen the panic in her eyes and refused to leave her. After all, nothing in the world outside was as terrifying to either of them as the thought of losing one another.

So the five children crept through the lawns and hedges towards the tower, each carrying one of the silver pistols which, George and CJ now knew, were specially designed stun guns that the Mortal Corps had built themselves, since normal guns were useless against immortals and none of them wanted to shoot a mortal person by accident.

From the little information they'd found on the omnicon, they knew the Castle was not heavily guarded. There was no security system to get through the doors, no cameras or keypads in the hallways; people could walk in and out of the building as they pleased. But the children knew it was dangerous to let anyone see them, so they moved swiftly and quietly, hiding behind pillars and statues and indoor plants whenever they heard footsteps or voices. Sophie was the best at this. She darted ahead of the others, around corners and along corridors and down flights of steps, keeping always within their field of vision, and never making a sound. George couldn't help but admire her surety and lightness of step; it was exactly the way he'd imagined a dancer or an acrobat might move.

There were surprisingly few people inside the Castle, and it did not take long to reach the cell block, which was located on the fifth basement level. The cell door required a code, which Hugo had found for them in Kingsley's message banks. George held his breath as Dragan entered the code. He could feel CJ trembling beside him – though whether with fear or excitement he did not know.

They opened the door.

"PAPA!" CJ shrieked.

The man in the chair looked up as she rushed to him, throwing her arms about his neck. "CJ?" His eyes were unfocussed, as though he'd just woken up.

"Papa," sobbed CJ, tightening her grip on him, "I was so scared when you were gone. I thought you were dead."

Papa's mouth twitched. "Never." He shifted in his seat, clearly wanting to embrace her but unable to, for he was shackled to the chair at the wrist, ankle, waist, and neck. CJ didn't seem to mind; she relaxed into him, and her sobbing quietened. Papa closed his eyes and a tear trickled down his cheek. He bent awkwardly to kiss the top of her head, murmuring, "My CJ, my Catherine…" After a moment his eyes opened, and he saw George standing in the doorway, too stunned to move.

"Papa," George choked, feeling tears well up in his own eyes. A part of him (small but insistent) had never really believed that they would see their father again. He was glad to let go of that part of himself now. Something inside him broke – and in the space of a breath he was at his father's side, his arms around Papa and CJ both, weeping with a mix of joy, relief, and the last dregs of fear.

The moment was short-lived. Dragan walked into the cell and examined the cold, metal restraints that held their father to the chair. He frowned. "Hugo didn't mention anything about this."

George looked at him, confused. "About what?"

Dragan tugged at one of the restraints, then gave a helpless shrug. "We've never seen someone tied to a chair before. Usually, Kingsley lets his prisoners move freely inside their cells. There's no keyhole or keypad. Hugo didn't say we'd have to untie anyone."

Panic gripped George around the throat. "You mean…you can't get Papa out of here?"

Before Dragan could answer, Tim and Sophie came in, looking grave.

"Empty," said Tim.

Dragan's eyes narrowed. "All of them?"

Tim and Sophie nodded.

"All of what?" CJ asked in a very small voice, looking around at everyone's faces.

Dragan took a step back, clenching his fists. "I had them check the other cells. There's no one else being held here. Dr LeVillain…where are the rest of your children?"

There was a silence, like the moment when a drop of water has just fallen from a leaky tap, and, having heard it, you wait to hear if it will drip again. And in that silence, George saw Dragan's question answered on Papa's face. A soundless scream tore itself from between his lips.

Then Sophie, standing by the door, looked out into the hallway and tensed. "People are coming," she hissed. "Lots of them. We need to leave *now.*"

Dragan nodded and started towards the door.

"Wait!" CJ yelled. "Not without Papa!"

Dragan shook his head and grasped her and George firmly by their shirt collars. He was only three or four years older than George, but much stronger, and George was still too much in shock to resist. The last thing he saw before he was dragged from the cell was his father, head lowered and shoulders heaving, his shackled body wracked with weeping.

■

They fought their way out of King's Castle within minutes. Tim and Sophie did most of the work, as Dragan had his hands full with hauling the hysterical LeVillain siblings along behind him. The Mortal Corps' stun guns were quick and effective, and both the Morans were a surprisingly good aim. It took less than fifteen minutes for the group to reach the space bridge, by which time they'd given Kingsley's agents the slip, and George had sufficiently recovered from shock to lose his temper with Dragan.

"Why wouldn't you save him?" he screamed, hot rage flaring inside him, burning away the last of his tears before they had the chance to escape his eyes. "You said you could help us! My brothers and sisters are *dead* – and Papa was right there – and you just *left* him!" He was so angry that he would have tried to strike the other boy, except that he was holding CJ tightly to his chest, while she buried her face in his jumper and cried.

Dragan took the onslaught calmly. "I'm sorry, George," he said. "This wasn't like our last two rescues. We didn't have enough time, and I wasn't going to risk the rest of us getting killed as well." He turned to the Morans, standing at the gate. "Ready, Tim?"

Tim nodded. "Ten seconds."

The space bridge activated, and a second later they were back in Olympus Mons, where they could see a vast plume of smoke rising in the distance, black against the naked sky. It was coming from the museum.

Dragan's eyes widened.

"*No.*"

■

Dr LeVillain was silent again by the time Aidan Kingsley walked through his cell door.

Kingsley paused, giving his friend a long look before he spoke. He was wearing a suit of pure white cashmere. His manner was pleasant, bordering friendly.

"So," he said. "There are more of them."

LeVillain merely twitched.

Kingsley's expression did not change. "How many, Raph?"

Twitch.

Kingsley sighed and snapped his fingers. LeVillain's body arched against the chair, limbs spasming, muscles straining against shackles that burned with thousands of volts. Raw screaming rent the air as every cell in his body was destroyed and replaced repeatedly at light speed.

After a minute or two, Kingsley snapped his fingers again and LeVillain flopped back against the chair, breathing heavily. A faint smell of burning filled the room, but there was not a mark on the prisoner's body.

"How many?" Kingsley repeated. His amicable expression had not moved, but there was something different about his tone, like a single shadow in a sunlit alleyway.

LeVillain made a harsh gasping sound that could, conceivably, have been laughter. "You won't break me, Aidan," he said. "Not now." The unspoken sentence hovered in the charred air between them: *Not now that I know they're alive.*

The corner of Kingsley's mouth turned down. "We'll see."

He snapped a third time and the screaming resumed. It echoed down the hallway as Kingsley turned and exited the cell, leaving the door open behind him.

■

They ran through the burning basement, calling frantically for Ajax, Hugo, Ruby, and Lewis, but there was no reply.

It was George who found Ajax face-down and motionless in the rubble, black uniform still smouldering against blackened skin. George stared numbly at the body, too exhausted to feel anything any more. A second later he heard a piercing cry, and turned weakly to see Dragan collapse by his brother's side, heedless of the flames that licked at him as he cradled the broken body in his arms.

George left them alone and joined the others, who were still searching desperately through the wreckage. But there was no sign of Hugo or the twins, and eventually the smoke forced them back underground.

They took shelter in a cavernous alcove at the end of an empty tunnel, huddling together in a miserable, shivering knot. Dragan was red-eyed and distraught. "I shouldn't have left," he kept sobbing. "It should have been me. I shouldn't have left. I shouldn't have left…" He soon lost coherence, burying his face in his hands. Sophie patted him timidly on the shoulder. For a long time, nobody spoke.

And then they heard a yell: "Timmy! Sophie!"

Everyone whipped around to see Ruby, Lewis, and Hugo racing up the tunnel towards them. The alcove erupted with a chorus of emotion: shock, relief, confusion, grief. Everyone hugged everyone else, garbled explanations were given, tears were shed, wounds were tended to.

It had been Ajax who had heard the intruders, Ajax who had sent the other three down into the sewers while he bought them time to hide. And it had been Ajax, of course, who had paid the ultimate price for his bravery.

Dragan and Hugo sat mutely together, mourning their brother's death. Watching them, George felt the last of his anger melt away. How could he blame Dragan for failing to help him and CJ now? It had been Dragan's willingness to help that had cost him the life of his own brother and the loss of his home.

George wasn't sure how to say it, but he locked eyes with Dragan, and they nodded once. No words were needed. In that moment they had made a declaration: someday, somehow, the Mortal Corps would bring an end to the Arcadian Empire forever.

Part Two

Chapter Eight

"Heads up!"

I look up from my breakfast as CJ throws me a shiny red apple. It's delivery day: a new shipment of supplies has come in. Tim jumps out of his seat and rushes to help her carry the enormous box. Together, they make their way through the dining hall, handing out snacks and sundries to those who requested them. Five years have passed since CJ and I joined the Mortal Corps, and I still have to marvel at the post-scarcity economy. None of us need to work for survival: we simply log onto the omnicon and order food, clothing, and other materials as needed, and they show up at the depot on the corner a day later.

I bite into the apple. It is sweet and crisp. "Thanks CJ," I yell with my mouth full.

She winks at me. At fifteen, she is beginning to look like a young woman. Although she is short for her age, she has spent the last few years bodybuilding and training in martial arts, and she walks with the quiet confidence of someone ten years her senior. For all that, she's as bright and lively on the inside as when she was a little child, before we lost Papa and the others. It took a long time for that side of her to reappear, but I am glad to see her back to her old self again.

CJ helps Tim set the supply box onto one of the big dining tables, and she hunts around inside it until she finds a smaller box. "Your parts are here, Hugo."

"Brilliant, thanks." Hugo takes the box from her and hurries away to his workshop. Over the last year, he's been modifying our stun guns to be able to target large groups of people at once, so that our overall military capacity will increase despite our low numbers.

That's not to say that our numbers haven't grown. Since the day we swore to destroy the Empire, we've staged many more rescues and increased our ranks to a little over a hundred. All of us are young; Dragan, at twenty, is still the oldest and the overall leader of the Corps. None of our new recruits can tell us what happened to their parents, which leads me and Dragan to believe that they have met the same fate as our fathers.

We've set up a new base on the fringes of the Empire, in a warehouse bordering the dark regions of Ganymede. There aren't many settlers out here. The nearest city, Terah Catena, is an hour away by lunar train. But that suits us just fine. We've acquired several more untraceable udevs, so we conduct most of our operations on the omnicon anyway. We've spent years tracking the Empire's resources and movements, slowly adding to our list of known immortal agents, and dropping subtly crafted propaganda into discussion forums in the deepest recesses of the omnicon, hoping that canny civilians will stumble across it and be drawn to sympathise with our cause.

I, however, along with Dragan, Tim, and several others, have created a false identity and re-entered Arcadian society. I hope to work my way into a position of power so I can get closer to Kingsley's inner circle. So, once I've eaten breakfast, I grab my udev and a book to read on the train, and I head out to the station.

No one has jobs any more, at least not in the sense of working for an employer and getting paid for it. Instead, people choose what they want to do with their time, and with a little help from the omnicon, they can advertise and distribute their goods and services as they please, essentially in exchange for social status. The jobs that no one wants to do are automated.

It took me a while to work out what I could do that might get me noticed by Kingsley, as there is very little about him on the omnicon, and nothing from the Empire resembling a mission statement or list of objectives. In fact, in terms of formal recorded history, there is nothing published, oncon or otherwise, after the year AD 1980. This is irritating, for it is hard to gauge the Empire's weaknesses when we know nothing of its formation or development save what we find on conspiracy sites hidden deep within the omnicon. Our new recruits haven't told us anything we didn't already know, since most of them were raised in the same sort of isolated conditions as CJ and me. However, a certain amount of cultural knowledge can be absorbed simply by spending time on the omnicon and seeing the sorts of things people say and do and take for granted. About a year ago, I concluded that Kingsley values infrastructure and land development, so I decided to become an architect.

It was slow going at first. Learning to use the software was tricky, as I'd never even used a udev before I was twelve. Then I had to take a couple of oncon courses to learn design principles. But the hardest part was figuring out what sort of design philosophy would appeal to Arcadian citizens and catch Kingsley's attention. After a few tries, I realised that Arcadian society values beauty over utility; and it's hard to have an instinct for beauty when you've spent most of your life locked up at home. But in the end, I got the hang of it.

I suppose my ignorance has been a help in many ways, because I've found a unique style that works for me and has garnered quite a lot of attention from the architecture community. I publish my designs under the pseudonym Angel Days, and my oncon profile has thousands of upvotes. Every few weeks, I get a new offer from some head of construction or other, asking to build one of my designs. But I've been holding out until someone from Arcadia makes me an offer, since the construction of a new building in the Empire's capital is sure to turn Kingsley's head.

Two days ago, I finally got what I wanted: a message from someone named Rosehip, expressing an interest in building one of my designs. I looked her up and found out that not only does she hail from Arcadia, but she's also Kingsley's Chief of Construction! It was an offer I couldn't refuse, and today I'm on my way to meet with her. I was surprised when she asked to meet in person; I'd assumed our negotiations would take place over the omnicon. But the more I see of the world, the more I come to realise that the standard of living set by Kingsley's immortal coterie is one of leisure and abundance, which does not naturally lend itself to cutting an experience short for the sake of convenience. In other words, why have a meeting over the omnicon when you can have one over lunch?

So I take the lunar train out to Terah Catena, and from there, the space bridge to Arcadia. It is nearly midday when I take my seat in the tiny boutique bar-cafe and wait for Rosehip to arrive. More out of habit than anything else, I check my udev. It's shaped like a silver wristwatch, and it generates a small holoscreen which I can use to access the omnicon. Not really my ideal design, but I got it second-hand, since ordering and registering a new one under my false name would lead to unnecessary complications. I look up Rosehip's profile and spend a few minutes browsing her construction portfolio, thinking that if I seem knowledgeable about her work, she'll be more likely to follow through with building my design.

At the appointed time, Rosehip enters the bar-cafe and takes a seat opposite me, smiling a greeting. She looks younger than I'd expected, probably only a few years my senior, and is dressed in a dark purple suede pantsuit. Her dark hair is artfully curled about her heart-shaped face, and she looks up at me with a pair of wide blue eyes so innocent you'd think she'd stepped straight out of a Tweety Bird cartoon. Despite her friendliness, I notice myself beginning to feel nervous.

"Angel Days?" she says.

I nod.

"Good to meet you. I'm Rosehip." She shakes my hand briskly, then pulls out her udev: a flat purple disc which matches her suit. "What are you thinking?"

It takes me a moment to realise she's talking about the lunch menu. I hasten to consult my own udev. "Er…probably the ricotta hotcakes. I'm a sweet tooth," I add hurriedly, though she does not appear fazed by my choice.

"Nice. I'm going to go with the breakfast roll." She taps a button and leans back in her chair, observing me. "So, how long have you been designing?"

"A few years," I hedge, not wanting to commit to any specific personal details in case she looks me up later. "How about you? Constructing, I mean."

She grins at me. "A few years." I can't tell if she's immortal. That's our biggest setback at the moment: we can't distinguish immortals from normal people, short of injuring them and waiting to see if they heal (an option we've rejected, for various reasons). Naturally, there are no records of which people Kingsley has promoted. "Long enough to get a feel for what this city needs. And right now…" She leans forward in her seat. "What it needs is an Angel Days original sky tower. Don't you agree?"

I can't help but return her smile. "I'd be more interested to know whether our good friend Aidan Kingsley agrees."

If she thinks me forward, she doesn't show it. "Fair question. I showed him your blueprint, as it happens. He was all for it." She winks. "Keep this up and you could get an official endorsement. Your upvotes would go through the roof."

Stunned at how easy it seems, I can only nod at her.

Presently, our food is brought to us, and we pass the rest of lunch dickering pleasantly over the finer details of the construction plan. I leave the meeting filled with excitement, satisfaction, and ricotta. *It's all coming together*, I think.

■

In a small room, a man in a white suit reaches out to push a big red button.

■

Over dinner, I relate my progress to Dragan. He claps me on the shoulder. He really likes doing that. "Attaboy, George. We'll have you in Kingsley's good graces in no time." He is smiling as he says it, but his eyes have clouded over. He's never really been the same since we lost Ajax. I don't blame him.

"How's the community?" I ask. This is what we call our propaganda strategy. It's far too dangerous even on the hidden omnicon to speak openly of overthrowing Kingsley and his immortals, so we share our ideas in the form of an omnicomic which we call Arcadence. Dragan and Ruby write it together and post it on all the underground media-sharing platforms, and several other Corps members use sockpuppet accounts to leave comments and upvotes, generating interest across the sites more broadly. As more and more civilians have begun to follow and upvote our content, we've built a whole fan community around Arcadence, which we hope to mobilise against the Empire when the time is right.

"We uploaded the new chapter a few hours ago," Dragan says. "Seven thousand upvotes so far. We're reaching the central climax soon."

"Have you written it out yet?"

"Only roughly. Ruby's working on it at the mo…" Dragan trails off, eyes narrowing as he turns to look at something behind me.

I follow his gaze to the opposite corner of the dining hall, where I can see several people standing, as if to attention. Closest to me is Ren Carter, one of our newest recruits. He is seventeen, and is usually a loud, boisterous personality. But in this moment, even at a distance, I can see an unusual rigidity in his stance, and a blankness on his face that makes my blood run cold.

People at neighbouring tables are turning to stare at him.

He pulls a gun from his jacket and opens fire.

Blood sprays across the wall – I can't tell whose. People are screaming. I am anchored to the ground. Beside me, Dragan leaps from his seat, shouting something I can't hear. My brain fogs over with panic. My gaze sweeps across the room, searching desperately for CJ. I see several others holding guns, but I barely notice them.

The smell of blood and gunpowder fills the air. My ears are pierced with screaming. I can't tell whose screams.

I think they're mine.

Chapter Nine

It doesn't take us long to subdue the traitors. There are ten of them, which still leaves nearly a hundred of us. But we were slow to react, and by the time they are all unconscious, they've killed or injured a quarter of our number.

Our leaders move swiftly into action. Tim and Sophie enlist help to disarm and bind the traitors. Ruby, Lewis, and CJ try to calm the rest of the group, tending to the injured and sending anyone who isn't needed to their bunks. Once the situation is under control, Dragan pulls me and Hugo into his private workroom for an emergency meeting.

"Sleeper agents," Hugo says, sensing his brother's question before he asks it.

Dragan nods. "Do we think anyone else could be compromised?"

"Hard to tell," I say. "Depends on if they acted knowingly or not. We'll have to interrogate them when they wake up. Until then, I wouldn't trust anyone we've recruited recently."

"I wouldn't trust anyone at all, except ourselves and the Morans," Hugo says. "We've come too far to let the Corps be destroyed from the inside."

I agree, though it hurts to admit it. I've become good friends with many of our new recruits. There are bonds you can only form through a sort of shared hardship and forced vulnerability. The thought that those bonds could be so easily broken causes a deep ache somewhere in my chest. "What are we going to do?" I ask.

"I don't know," Dragan says, "but we can't play the long game any more. If the gunners were with Kingsley, then we don't know how much he knows about us. Our base could be compromised – he could have people spying on all our operations. And even if he isn't, we can't have tension and distrust eating away at everybody for the next ten years. We have to act now, while Kingsley thinks we're still recovering from the shock."

"I agree, but what are we going to *do*?" I repeat, shocked at the level of anger I can hear in my own voice.

Dragan scowls at me. "I *said* I don't know. But give me twenty-four hours and I'll figure it out." He slumps into the chair at his desk, and I leave the room.

■

In the interim, we mourn the dead: Rufus, Harper, Jaxon, Riza, Ami, Lachlan, Dia, Stefano, Moses, Kristof, and Sara. We tend the sick, clean up the mess, and spend time alone or with others in quiet contemplation. Sophie, Tim, CJ and I conduct a thorough search of the base for any more hidden weapons. We find nothing. Hugo continues working on his modified stun guns. Ruby and Lewis monitor the omnicon for further signs of trouble on the horizon. And Dragan keeps to his workroom, without eating or sleeping or speaking.

Around the tenth hour, our captives begin to wake. It falls to me to interrogate them. So, I walk slowly into the room where Ren Carter is kept, tied down to a chair. It reminds me unpleasantly of when we went to try and rescue Papa. I push that thought away and look at Ren for a moment. He stares back at me with that same blank expression he wore last night when he shot Ami through the head.

I am silent for a long time. I don't really know what to say. I've never done something like this before.

Finally, I speak, keeping my voice as calm as I can. "Is it really you, Ren?"

He just looks at me, unblinking.

"Am I talking to Ren Carter, or are you just some mindless drone controlled by Kingsley?" I ask. "Is there even a difference?"

The faintest smile tugs at the corner of his mouth. He doesn't utter a word, but that smile says it all: he knew exactly what he was doing last night.

I take a deep breath. "I thought you were my friend, Ren. I really like you. We've had so many good conversations, and you're always kind to CJ. You're like——" I stop, as something inside me clenches tight. My chest feels hot. I force myself to continue. "You're like my brother Marcus. Before he was killed. By people like you."

His smile fades, but there isn't a hint of remorse in his cold grey eyes. "You're all going to die anyway. What's the use of being upset about it?"

"Are you immortal?" I ask.

He just smirks at me. "You really don't know anything, do you?"

"I know enough," I say, and pull the knife I brought with me out of my pocket.

He grits his teeth as I drag the blade across his palm, drawing blood, but shows no other signs of pain. Then I watch as the wound closes again without leaving even a scar – only the blood that has already been spilled, smudged upon his palm. Clear proof that he's in league with Kingsley.

"You're lucky," I say, wiping the blade on his shirt. "That's the only thing stopping us from killing you, like you killed Ami." I turn to leave, then pause as a thought occurs to me. "Not that we couldn't give it a try, of course."

Even in my anger, I don't really mean it. But I hope the threat will scare him enough to make him think about what he's done.

■

A brief, bloody investigation reveals that the nine other traitors are immortals like Ren, but everyone else among our ranks is mercifully normal. I suppose merely being mortal doesn't guarantee that a person's loyalties lie outside the Empire, but that, combined with the lack of any other weapons found, is enough for me to step back and breathe a bit easier.

At the appointed hour, I meet with Dragan and the other leaders. Dragan appears not to have left his desk since yesterday, but he shows none of the same weariness as before. He looks up at us with bright determination, and we can feel the energy rising in the air.

Dragan speaks without preamble. "We have to take the fight directly to Kingsley." He pauses for the space of half a breath – then, when it is apparent that none of us are going to say anything, he continues. "If we move now, we could capture King's Castle in a matter of hours. He won't be expecting an attack. I had Hugo contact him via Ren Carter's udev to say that the traitors have wiped most of us out and are hunting the last survivors down. Even if he catches on that it wasn't Carter who sent the message, all our strategies thus far have been long-term, so if the traitors have kept him informed of our movements, he'll think we're still working towards uncovering the identities of all his immortals. With the element of surprise on our side, we can physically incapacitate him and use him as leverage to get the rest of the immortals to surrender. I know it's a big risk, but we can't afford to wait any longer."

There is an impressive silence.

"Do you really think we can do it?" asks Sophie.

Dragan shrugs. "They might have weapons now, but none of the traitors had any protection against our stun guns, which probably means the Castle guards won't either. And even if they do, there's never more than a couple of dozen people inside King's Castle at one time. We can overwhelm them with sheer numbers if we have to. Anyway," he says fiercely, "it's better than sitting around here, waiting for them to finish us off."

He looks each one of us in the eye as he speaks. If anyone has misgivings, they do not voice them. Each of us knows that this is a crazy idea. But Dragan's confidence is infectious. When I look at him, I feel a wild hope burning within me. And at the end of the day, I think he's right: what other options do we have?

I grin at him. "You're the leader," I say. "Let's do it."

Chapter Ten

Dusk has fallen over Arcadia by the time we march on King's Castle. All of us are here, save the youngest and the most seriously injured – nearly seventy in total. We move swiftly and purposefully, but there is no one around to notice us as we charge towards the colossal building.

The doors are locked, but not guarded. We force them open using several small explosive devices which Hugo has prepared for just such an occasion. Inside the atrium there are five guards carrying rifles. We knock them to the ground using one of our modified stun guns before they have a chance to react. Even with their immortal bodies and newly-acquired weaponry, they haven't trained for combat like we have.

Once the atrium is secure, we split off into several groups to cover the rest of the building. Dragan, CJ and I head directly for the top floor, where, our intelligence tells us, Kingsley's office is located. He should be in at this hour; even if he isn't, there's a lot we can do with just his tools.

The superlift crackles and hums as it rockets up towards the 200th floor. We reach the top in under five minutes and burst out the doors, weapons at the ready.

I don't know what I was expecting to find up here, but it certainly wasn't this. The 200th floor is all one giant pyramidal room, with slanting glass walls through which you can see what seems like the entire country laid out in every direction like a bed of jewels. The room is almost like a library, with mazes of long, low shelves crammed full of beautiful books, snaking along the floor in an intricate pattern. The shelves are covered with ivy vines and topped with potted plants of varying shapes, colours, and sizes. At the centre of the room, a large, round section of floor dips into a shallow fishpond, and in the centre of that stands a towering cherry-willow tree, trailing branches in full blossom which sway gently in the artificial breeze. A number of brightly coloured birds are perched amongst the blossoms, softly fluting a melody that sounds eerily like "Ode to Joy."

In the midst of this peculiar paradise there stands a young man in a white linen suit who can only be Aidan Kingsley, gazing at us with an expression that is curious, expectant, but not the least bit surprised or afraid.

During the couple of seconds it takes me to register all this, I also notice that not only is Kingsley completely alone, but he does not appear to be armed or protected in any way. I am tempted to assume this is sheer stupidity on his part; but as I meet his eye for the first time, I can see the truth: he genuinely does not consider any of us a threat. It's as simple as that. Nothing will convince him that his reign will ever be shaken. He is absolute. He is king.

The sheer arrogance of this man infuriates me more than I can understand, and before anyone can speak a word, I open fire, aiming for his head.

He steps casually out of range, light as a dancer.

I fire again, with the same result.

He smiles lazily at me.

The three of us launch a volley of stun bolts, moving in on him as quickly as we can while keeping our aim steady. He dodges every attack with the same effortless grace, jumping up onto shelves and darting in between the pots and plants without knocking anything so much as an inch out of place. When we get close enough, he springs into the air over our heads, landing right behind us.

We turn too late. I catch a glimpse of metal, and suddenly Dragan has fallen to his knees, his face contorted with agony, bright flecks of crimson spraying from his kidney onto the shelf behind him. Kingsley has already darted back out of the way; not a single drop of Dragan's blood has touched his clothing.

I scream wordlessly and launch myself at him, as CJ does the same. He fends us off successfully for several minutes, but he has made a crucial error: he assumes that Dragan is already dead. And the moment Kingsley pauses for breath, back turned to his would-be victim, Dragan weakly raises his weapon, takes careful aim, and fires. Kingsley's smile freezes on his face. His limbs go slack, and he crumples to the ground, unconscious.

■

By the time Kingsley wakes, he is tied down to the same chair that once held my father. King's Castle has fallen, and Dragan is dead.

CJ and I have been guarding the cell for the last few hours. The others are busy securing the rest of the prisoners and barricading the Castle against further intrusion. While Kingsley was unconscious, I worked out how to activate the mechanism in the chair that electrocutes the occupant. The thought of Kingsley and his friends doing that to my father sickens me. I leave the mechanism alone for now.

He looks at me and smiles, silently mocking. He still thinks he has nothing to fear from me. I think about activating the mechanism, but can't quite bring myself to do it.

I am still working out what to say to him when CJ asks, "Why did you take our papa and the rest of our family away?" The words sound childish, but when I look at her, I see only the flat, hard anger of a grown-up, and I know Kingsley sees it too.

He shrugs as best as he can beneath the restraints. "They threatened the stability of my empire, so they had to be removed."

"Your empire is going to fall very soon anyway," I say, "and there's nothing you can do to save it. Once we capture the last of your immortals and show how pathetic your way of life really is, the rest of the population will stop trying to pander to you and your petty whims, and your reign will be over."

Kingsley's smile fades at that, and for a moment I think I have finally shaken him. But then he bursts out laughing – not maniacally, like so many of the villains I've read about in stories, but the easy, honest laughter of a person overcome with mirth. It strikes me for the first time how young he looks – only a year or two older than me, at most. Yet beneath that youthful exterior his mind is ancient, cynical and warped. It's probably been decades since he last laughed like this.

"You really don't know anything, do you?" he says at last, gasping for breath. "You really think that I and a handful of immortals have this huge mortal population under our thumbs? What, did you read about that on some conspiracy site? Let me guess, it was Archangel. Or – no, VNews. Am I getting close?"

Neither of us says anything, but he can read it on our faces. He starts laughing again, shaking helplessly as if in pain.

"I *know* the people who run those sites!" he says. "They aren't conspiracy theorists, they just get off on pretending – seeing how close they can spin their web of irony to the truth. Everyone who follows them knows it's a joke, and they play along with it because it kills some time. I'm sorry you failed to see the funny side of it. Really, you've no idea what you were missing."

I hate being talked down to. I can feel my fingers twitch, itching to pull that trigger, to make him suffer for everything he's done. But I resist. If we keep him in a good mood, he'll be more likely to tell us what we want to know.

"I don't understand you," I say at last. "Are you saying immortality isn't real?"

Kingsley's laughter subsides, and he looks at me for a moment with something very close to pity. "You poor boy," he says. "Your father is one of the smartest men alive, and he still couldn't teach you to add two and two together. Of *course* immortality is real! *Everyone* is immortal! *You* brats are the only ones in the Empire who will ever die, and you think you can topple it just by strapping me to a chair and making some pretty speeches? Forgive me if I find myself unconvinced." He starts chuckling again.

Anger and shock chase each other in circles inside me. I don't know what to say, what to think, what to do. Everyone immortal? Except us? How? Why? What —

CJ touches my arm. Her hand is warm and comforting. I begin to relax.

"Tell us everything," she says.

Kingsley laughs. "That's a good girl. My, but I'd forgotten what it was like to thirst for knowledge. I do miss it, I'll admit——"

"Just shut up and answer her," I snap, fed up with his condescension.

He shrugs. "There's not much to tell. Once upon a time, I discovered infinite cellular regeneration: immortality. I was willing to share my gift with the world, on condition that its governance should fall to me. Some people accepted. Others died. Eventually the only people left were those who shared my vision. And so, the immortal generation was born. Of course, we only accepted those who were young, strong, and healthy; we weren't so cruel as to inflict perpetual suffering on the elderly and infirm. Healthy children were allowed to grow to the age of eighteen before undergoing the treatment. The rest…were allowed to enjoy what little life they had remaining. So it went, until there were no children left – for we couldn't very well keep on reproducing if no one was to die. So the treatment was designed to render the patient sterile, and finally, we were left as one perfect, eternal generation, free to roam the universe as we wished, until the end of time. But you see, that's where you come in. Your father, if we can call him that, is a brilliant man, but a sentimental fool. After years – decades – *centuries* of enjoying his life and scientific pursuits, he decided to reject the gift he'd been given. He believed that life and death are necessary opposites, or some nonsense like that. And so, he and his misguided friends manufactured a new wave of *mortal* humans: you."

We stare at him, unable to process what he's saying. "Papa…*manufactured* us?" I say.

"Of course he did," Kingsley says impatiently. "No one can have children naturally any more. Didn't you ever wonder why you don't have a mother? Raphael LeVillain isn't really your father, any more than you are really brother and sister. You're *clones*. He built you out of tiny pieces of himself and *pretended* you were his children, as though that would do you any good. You and all your filthy mortal friends are nothing more than the pathetic pet-projects of a group of weak-minded traitors."

"You're lying," I say faintly. But deep down, I know he isn't. We never did know anything about our mother. And people were always so shocked when we spoke to them, as though they'd never seen a child before…

Beside me, CJ is shaking with suppressed rage. "Even if that's true," she says through gritted teeth, "even if we aren't normal, what was the harm in us being created? Why couldn't you just let us live our lives in peace?"

"Because," says Kingsley, "Arcadian society is founded on the truth that everyone will live forever. It's been long enough now that most people have forgotten they were mortal to begin with. If they see you, and remember, there's no telling how many may regret their immortality and seek for a way to reverse the treatment. If they found it…Arcadia would fall. Everything I've built would be for nothing."

"But you can't *really* believe that you'll live forever!" CJ nearly shouts with frustration. "The universe itself will end one day! Do you really think that your infinite cellular whatever will protect you from that?"

Kingsley shrugs again. "By the time that happens, we'll have worked out a way to survive. We might even be able to create our *own* universe by then."

"But you can't just go on *forever*," I protest. "Every story needs an ending! That goes for human lives as well!"

Kingsley looks up at me and smiles a gentle smile.

"But we do have an ending," he says. "'And they all lived happily ever after.'"

Chapter Eleven

With Dragan gone, we naturally look to Hugo to lead our campaign against the Empire, since he was privy to all his brother's plans. Hugo, however, has always preferred to be a background player, and he asks Tim, Sophie, CJ, and me to help him plan our next move.

It is decided that Hugo and CJ will remain at King's Castle with the majority of our troops, to hold off any retaliatory actions from the Arcadians, and eventually – we hope – to negotiate a peace treaty. The Morans and a few others will return to home base to protect our young and injured comrades. And I will lead a small team on an expedition to the dwarf planet Pluto, where, Kingsley tells me, our parents are being held in a secret prison. There has never been any mention on the omnicon of human beings travelling further than the moons of Jupiter, much less colonising Pluto. But when Kingsley told me, he wore that same mocking smile and assured me that my father had no more ability to bring down the Empire than I did. It seems to me that a man with that much confidence would have little reason to lie.

We take one of Kingsley's private spacecraft, big enough to hold fifty passengers plus fuel. It is a long, uneventful journey out to Pluto. We don't hear anything from the rest of the Corps, but I assume they aren't having too much trouble. From what I've observed, it seems that Kingsley and his small group of agents are the backbone of Arcadian law enforcement; the rest of the Empire's citizens are too absorbed in their own lives to care much about external events. And there is no military, of course.

When we finally move in for landing, I can see a long, low building set into the distant foothills which I can only assume is the prison, for there are no other structures in sight, nor roads, nor any other signs of civilisation. The icy surface below us tells me that the planet hasn't even been terraformed, which means we won't be able to breathe outside. The spacecraft isn't equipped with any moonsuits or gravity simulators either, since immortals – whose bodies will regenerate at a faster speed than cold or pressure or oxygen deprivation can damage them – presumably terraform out of aesthetic sensibility rather than necessity.

I curse under my breath as I fumble with the controls, trying to alter our course so that we land directly adjacent to the prison. If we get close enough, we should be able to extend one of the airlock chutes into the building and enter that way. I hope the walls aren't reinforced.

It's not a pretty landing, but it does the job. A thought occurs to me, and I open my udev, turning as I do so to one of my crew, instructing him to take control of the airlock chute. I run a brief search of Kingsley's message banks – a significantly easier task now, since Hugo broke the encryption on the system soon after we captured King's Castle. It takes a bit of digging, but eventually I find the original blueprint for the prison, which informs me that the building itself is usually depressurised (to ensure maximum discomfort for the prisoners), but can be pressurised within ten minutes if the command key is entered from an authorised udev.

I send a message back to King's Castle, and soon receive a reply from Sophie, informing me that an authorised udev has been confiscated and the command key entered. I wait fifteen minutes, just to be sure, then head down the airlock chute, which has now been driven into the prison wall. I close the airlock behind me and take a deep breath as I prepare to open the forward door, knowing that if the building hasn't been pressurised, I will die almost instantly.

The door opens.

I don't die.

■

We split into pairs to cover more ground. Cell block by cell block, we incapacitate the guards, release the prisoners, and instruct them to wait for us back at the spacecraft. We have freed nearly the entire prison by the time I find Papa, sitting chained to a wall and staring blankly into the corner of his cell, completely motionless except for the odd twitch.

I break the chains with one of Hugo's mini detonators and pull him upright. He stares at me, eyes glazed over with confusion and shock. "Are you…George?"

I am suddenly conscious of how much taller I've grown in the last five years. Papa, on the other hand, looks exactly the same as he did when I was small. I've never realised this before, but he looks...young. He couldn't have been more than twenty when he became immortal. I picture myself growing old and dying someday, while he stays like this forever. I feel a sharp pain in my chest, and my eyes grow hot.

"Why didn't you tell us what we were?" I choke. "Why keep us locked away all those years and not even tell us what we were hiding from?"

Tears spill down Papa's face, and he wraps his arms around me. I make no move to reciprocate. "I'm so sorry, George," he says into my shoulder. "I just wanted you to have a happy childhood. I know I hurt you, but I loved you too much to tell you the truth. I really did think of you all as my children. What father could tell his children they are hated by the world?"

I don't know how to answer that question, but the rage in me dims, and my chest stops aching. I put my arms around him, and after a long moment, we turn and wordlessly exit the cell.

■

During the voyage back to Earth, I explain as best as I can to our new guests the events which have transpired since they were arrested. They are jubilant, apprehensive, grief-stricken, and sombre by turns. The worst is when I have to tell Antony Smith about Ajax and Dragan's deaths. But eventually everyone is able to process all I have told them, and we arrive in Arcadia without any trouble.

On entering King's Castle, we are received with open arms, and there is a celebration to balance out the tragedies of late. Clones and creators – children and parents – embrace each other joyfully, and a contingent is sent off to Ganymede to be reunited with our comrades back at home base.

When the excitement has died down, I meet with Hugo, CJ, and our respective fathers in one of Kingsley's many private rooms. "Well done on the Pluto trip, George," Hugo says, taking my hand in both his own. He seems dazed. I don't blame him; losing one's brother and shortly thereafter regaining a long-lost father will do that to anybody.

"Thanks," I say. "So, what have I missed?"

Hugo looks grim. "It's going to be harder than we thought to find a peaceable way out of this mess. Kingsley won't give us the time of day, and it turns out the apathetic Arcadian masses aren't quite so apathetic when their leader is forcibly removed from his throne. If enough of them turn violent, there's no telling how much firepower they might be able to muster against us, given the time and resources."

I frown. "Then we need some leverage."

"That goes without saying, but what do we use?" asks CJ. "They already have everything they could ever want, and there's nothing they're afraid of. We've no carrot, and no stick."

"The Genesis Circle," Papa says suddenly. We all look at him. "A while back, maybe a hundred years or so, there was a small group of people who'd come to hate their immortality, and they sought a way to end their lives. The Genesis Circle was what they called themselves, since they believed that life should have a beginning and an end. I knew a few of them back then. I shared some of their beliefs, although I took them in a...different direction." He says the last part almost bashfully, avoiding eye contact with me and CJ.

"The Genesis Circle disbanded half a century ago, Raph," says Antony. "What's your point?"

"My point," says Papa, "is that Aidan Kingsley hinted to me a few years ago that the Circle may still be active – or at the very least, their findings might still be out there somewhere. If we can figure out where to look, we might just be able to find ourselves a weapon that could kill an immortal." He smiles wryly. "What better leverage could you ask for?"

Chapter Twelve

Papa and Antony search tirelessly for the last remnants of the Genesis Circle. This mainly involves sending long, convoluted chains of o-mails back and forth with colleagues of yesteryear, which I am reluctant to get involved with, since I still find it difficult to think about my father's earlier life, and all that led up to my creation.

■

We maintain tight control of King's Castle, and slowly begin to occupy some of the other strongholds scattered throughout the Empire. Small bands of Arcadians try to fight back, with very little to their advantage save their inability to die. I grow to hate the violence with a deep, visceral hatred. I can feel the stress eating away at my insides at the end of every battle.

■

"Why won't you just give up?" I ask Kingsley in his cell one day.

He looks at me but says nothing.

"Your ideas will never prevail," I say, more confidently than I feel. "Sooner or later, the people of Arcadia are going to realise that everything you stand for, everything you've done to people like me, is wrong. Your empire is going to crumble eventually, so why not dissolve it now, while you still have a chance of being forgiven?"

But Kingsley acts as if he doesn't hear anything I say. When I turn and leave the cell, I can hear his laughter echoing through the hall behind me.

■

"I think it's time we publish the Epilogue," Hugo says to me, after another skirmish with the Arcadian guerrillas has bled to an end, leaving six more of our comrades dead.

The Epilogue is a written document which constitutes the final chapter of our omnicomic, Arcadence. It explains the ideas and intentions behind the entire story, drawing parallels between the characters in the comic and our own Mortal Corps, and elaborating on the themes of life, death, compassion, and justice which have underpinned the narrative since its beginning. We've held off publishing it until now, but have always hoped that, when the time was right, it would help us garner sympathy from the comic's fan community.

I'm not sure I agree with Hugo that the time is now, but desperation has been gnawing at me for so long that I no longer trust my own instincts.

I nod wearily. "Maybe you're right."

We publish the Epilogue an hour later, and the omnicon is thrown into uproar: a howling, contradictory chaos of protests, manifestos and opinions thrown carelessly into the void.

I begin to wonder if I will ever feel any sort of faith in humanity again.

■

Towards the end of the fifth week, we hold a leaders' meeting, during which Papa and Antony come to us bearing good news.

"We've struck gold," says Papa, smiling despite the dark circles beneath his eyes. He and I look so similar, it makes my heart ache. He unrolls the blueprint he is carrying under one arm, and hands it to Hugo with a flourish. "We managed to get in contact with Freya Holmes, one of the original members of the Genesis Circle. I met her back when I was still going to their meetings. She gave us the planning documents for a molecular pulse ray which the Circle designed. They never actually built it, but theoretically, it would be strong enough to counteract infinite cellular regeneration and destroy an immortal person on the spot. They called it the Ultimatum."

"So dramatic," mutters CJ.

Papa chuckles. "I mean, they called themselves the *Genesis Circle.*"

"True."

Hugo is reading through the blueprint, frowning slightly. "This thing is a feat of bioterrorism, that's for sure. Seems tricky to put together, though."

"If it were easy, someone would have built it before now," Antony says gently. "Do you think you can do it?"

Hugo's frown deepens for a moment. Then he looks up and grins suddenly. "Not only could I do it, but I could do it on a mass scale if we can get hold of the resources. Heck, give me enough time and I could modify this design and make it into a WMD. That would make the Arcadians take notice, I bet."

"You're not suggesting we kill *all* the immortals?" I say, aghast. While there is little love lost between myself and Arcadian society, the thought of committing an outright genocide is appalling to me, and I can tell that the others in the room agree.

"Of course not," Hugo replies, frown returning. "But if they know that's what we're capable of, then they'll hardly resist any longer, will they?"

There is a long pause.

"I don't know, Hugo," I say at last. "I don't like the idea of forcing a person to do something under threat of death. I mean, that's basically what Kingsley tried to do to us, and that's why we turned against him in the first place. To do that to an entire population…"

"Well, what else *can* we do?" Hugo snaps. The sudden force in his tone startles me, as he is usually so quiet. For a fleeting moment, I can see the raw hatred in his eyes, finally bubbling up to the surface after so many years filled with fear, pain, and loss. Then it is gone. "If you have ideas, I'm willing to hear them," he says wearily. "But I will do what it takes to defend our family, even if that means using the Ultimatum."

Silence weighs on the room, sliding down my throat like poison, choking me. My head hurts, my hands are cold. I don't have the strength to argue any more.

"But that's it!" CJ shouts. In response to our stares, she continues: "Ultimatum means choice, doesn't it? That's what we need – to give them the choice! If it's possible to destroy an immortal body instantaneously on the molecular level, then surely it's possible just to *alter* the body on that same level – not to kill the person, but to make them mortal again, like a reversal of the original operation? If we could do that, we could offer people the choice: become mortal like us, and embrace a new way of life – or stay the way they are and be content with that. If we give them that choice, when Kingsley has hidden it from them for so long, there's no way they'd stay loyal to him over us! Everyone wins, nobody gets killed."

As she finishes triumphantly, a new energy fills the room.

"CJ," Hugo says slowly, "you might just be right."

Papa smiles. "That's my girl."

■

In time, the dust settles. The Arcadian guerrillas eventually realise they won't be able to defeat us without some serious military force, and the fighting comes to an uneasy standstill. Aidan Kingsley is sent into exile on Pluto. The ruckus on the omnicon starts to die down, and we draw in a collective deep breath.

In the midst of this fleeting peace, Papa and his team of scientists finally unravel the secrets of cellular regeneration. I'm not in the room when the moment of breakthrough occurs, but I hear the stories about it afterwards, and am told that somebody (perhaps Papa) did, in fact, shout 'Eureka'.

∎

Once the Mortality Project is declared successful, the foundations of Arcadian thought begin to crumble – imperceptibly at first, then in a great cataclysm that ripples through the solar system. All across the Empire, people are grappling with the notion of death, and whether it could be something to be desired. Even the idea of it seems to cause them such immense, conflicting emotions. Having never had this choice myself, I cannot begin to imagine what it must be like for them. After a while, I have to ban myself from following the arguments on the omnicon; the whirling eddies of popular opinion are too much for my exhausted mind to handle.

One morning, however, I am standing on a quiet street at the edge of the city, looking up at the skyline and envisioning a building I am going to create someday, when I notice someone standing beside me. I turn to see a woman – who knows her real age? – looking at me with tears in her eyes.

"You're one of them, aren't you?" she says. "One of those…people who can die?"

I say nothing.

"I recognise you from the newscasts," she says. "You took Aidan Kingsley prisoner. You want everybody to die, like you."

I shake my head. "No," I say. "I want everybody to live. Aidan Kingsley wanted people like me to die.

He killed my brothers and sisters. So we had to fight him, so that we could be allowed to live alongside you. We had to make mortality an option so that people like us could be normal, not hunted down like animals. But that doesn't mean everybody has to die. You don't, if you don't want to."

She looks down.

"I don't know what I want," she whispers.

I smile at her. "That's okay," I say. "You have eternity to think about it."

■

In time, the first wave of immortals demanding to be 'cured' comes knocking at our doors. I have despised them for so long without fully knowing it that I am shocked to find myself moved by the fear, the determination, the peacefulness in each person's eyes. I want to ask them why they have come here, but am afraid of what their answers might stir up in me.

■

Our leaders meet with the Arcadian representatives who have stepped up to fill the void left by Kingsley, and a peace treaty is negotiated.

■

Time passes, people age and die, and children are born.

Life continues.

Epilogue

Eighty years have passed. Papa is long dead, but I have yet to undertake that journey for myself. I got married a few years after the Mortality Project ended and the Corps dissolved. I am a father myself now, and a grandfather, and even a great-grandfather. I have spent my life caring for my family and creating beautiful things, and I am happy with how it all turned out.

CJ died a year ago, and I mourned her loss bitterly, and I still do. But I look at her life, and I can see a certain beauty in its completion. I would never have grasped the full extent of my love for her if I hadn't lost her. Or perhaps this is just what I tell myself, so I can keep believing we were right.

I feel myself growing weaker, and I know my turn is coming soon. I lie in my bed surrounded by family and friends, and I can see the grief pre-emptive on their faces. My wife sits beside me and takes my hand in hers. I have never felt my own preciousness in the eyes of others reflected back to me so clearly.

I look out the window, and I can see the sun breaking through the clouds, and I take a deep breath – and smile.

About the Author

Eilidh Direen is a Tasmanian author who can't decide if she is a town mouse, a country mouse, or a street rat. She enjoys sunshine, nature, pub crawls, grub crawls (where you only go to grubby pubs), memes, and volleyball. Her motto is "Choccy milk tastes better when you drink it with friends."